A Black Girl's Blues
Part II

In the Midst of Darkness,
Blue Skies Lie Ahead

Published by ZL Publishing House
Book Cover Design by Stacy Day

A CIP catalog record for this book is available from the Library of Congress.

Stacy Day
    A Black Girl's Blues/ by Stacy Day

To contact the author, please visit: www.authorstacyday.com

ISBN-13: 978-1-7339974-9-2 (paperback)

Made in the USA
10 9 8 7 6 5 4 3 2 1

A Black Girl's Blues
Part II

In the Midst of Darkness, Blue Skies Lie Ahead

Stacy Day

PUBLISHING
HOUSE

Contents

Acknowledgments

I would like to thank my family and friends for your love and support throughout the release of Part I edition of *A Black Girl's Blues: In the Midst of Darkness, Blue Skies Lie Ahead*. I give a big "thank you" to my relatives here in Houston, Texas, and Lafayette, Louisiana who have been so supportive in showing their eagerness to purchase and promote my book. Also, I would like to thank everyone for coming out to my book release party for Part I and making it a big success; thank you all for not only purchasing my book, but also my merchandise as well.

To my beautiful sisters, Sherena, Temetris, and Kimberly, thank ya'll for your support in keeping Part I of *A Black Girl's Blues* alive in continuing to do promotion on your social media accounts.

To my wonderful children, Ahmad and Ahmari, thank you for being patient when I ask for "me time" to put my creative skills to work. Also, I would like to give a special thank you to my husband, Ahmad Day; You and I may not always see things eye-to-eye, but you always give me the love and encouragement needed to stay strong in my faith when I am faced with adversity.

To my darling mother, thank you. Although she passed away four years ago now, I know she would be very proud of me for being steadfast on my journey to become a successful writer. Also, I would like to thank my father aka "Dad" for being attentive and having those long talks with me about taking this book to the big screen.

I would like to acknowledge my friend, Nicole Jackson, who I have known since high school. I playfully call her my

"Life coach" because of how inspiring she has been in my life. And, I thank William T. Hoston for your amazing editorial skills in Part II of **A Black Girl's Blues**. Last, but certainly not least, I can't forget about my Lord and Savior upstairs for giving me the breath of life and blessing me with the opportunities to make my goals come to pass.

About Me

Stacy Day was born and raised in Houston, Texas. She managed to work a full-time job throughout her duration in college as she obtained an Associates in Arts degree with emphasis in Early Childhood Education from Houston Community College System; she then continued her education at the University of Houston where she graduated with a Bachelors of Science in Sociology degree.

She began writing unpublished short stories at the age of 16-years-old and later became inspired to write her own novel after reading Author Sister Souljah's novel "The Coldest Winter Ever." Later a friend handed her a book to read by author Terry McMillan titled, "A Day Late and a Dollar Short." It was then she read several more books by the author that sparked a flame in her soul that brought out her passion to begin a secondary career as an author.

Synopsis of *A Black Girl's Blues*, Part I

A Black Girl's Blues (2019) is a literary fictional novel with a subtlety of characters. Part I begins with the main character, Mia Harris, who is a savvy young woman. As a single mother, Mia's life choices have been contentious based on her own selfish needs. Her life has maneuvered through tumultuous relationships with family and the men in her life.

Mia manipulates men by using her beauty and sexuality to get what she wants. A ride or die chick, she rides for the wrong men and the expected outcomes define her life.

Synopsis of *A Black Girl's Blues*, Part II

A Black Girl's Blues, Part II (2021) begins with Colleen, the mother, and Jazzman, the daughter, who are attempting to get to the core of their unresolved issues with each other. Colleen is not the perfect mother. Her past drug addiction, conflated with one of her ex-boyfriend's sexually abusing Jazzman, has caused much pain in their mother-daughter relationship.

Mia continues the error of her ways with a series of bad decisions that later leads her to a physical confrontation with Claude, the father of her unborn child. Meanwhile, she has told her new man, Brad, he is the father.

Meanwhile, Makayla and Roxy continue to fight to keep their love alive. One is madly in love, and the other is in lust—a mismatched formula for success. In Part II, the family of women are learning from their past mistakes in their quest to better themselves and lead drama-free lives.

Therapy Session

C OLLEEN, THE MOTHER, and Jazzman, the daughter, both sat patiently waiting for the therapist to enter the room before greetings commenced.

Once inside, the therapist asked, "How is everything going, Colleen and Jazzman?"

"We are fine," said both mother and daughter simultaneously. Both women looked at each other with the same half-smile in unison.

"Well, I am glad that you both were able to come today," said Dr. Langston, sounding very energetic and happy to see them. "Have you been communicating with one another since our last session?" Her question broached the air of the moment.

"I just got married recently, and Jazzman came to the reception," said Colleen. "We didn't have much time to talk privately, but we were cordial with one another," she told the therapist.

"We have been busy doing our own thing," said Colleen while taking a glance at her daughter as she explained. "My husband and I just moved into our new home, and Jazzman has been working part-time. Also, she just started culinary classes at the community college."

"Congratulations to you, Colleen, on the wedding," noted Dr. Langston with a smile! "I am so happy for the both of you."

"Jazzman, this is great that you found a direction that you want to follow now," said Dr. Langston. "What made you want to pursue the culinary arts field?"

"I love cooking and experimenting with different foods in the kitchen," answered Jazzman. "It's a very good profession that could pay very well."

Dr. Langston really felt that this session would be much better than the last one. She thought they were showing progress sooner than she had expected, judging from their facial expressions and body mannerisms. Each appeared to be in a great mental space. And Dr. Langston was crossing her fingers inside of her mind that Colleen and Jazzman would keep up their calm and collect demeanors. "Sounds like the perfect start to figuring out your future plans."

"Yeah, I hope to own my own restaurant one day," added Jazzman.

"Alright...so far, I like the progress that's been made between the both of you. It's very good life-changing moves," stated the therapist. Dr. Langston was proud to see that the ladies' personal lives were improving as well. Despite progress, she still wanted the two to communicate more as increased communication would help to reestablish a strong bond. She expressed to them: "I would like for the both of you to start talking more outside of these sessions."

"Don't worry, this will not be an overnight process, but it's going to take some effort on both of your parts if you want to cultivate a better relationship," she told them. In agreement, Colleen responded, "I will definitely start doing my part to make sure that our relationship is mended." Her response was sincere and genuine. As the mother, she had to lead by example regardless of the past fracture in their relationship.

"Okay, I'm going to hold you to your word," Dr. Langston told them. "But, in order for that to work, you must put in the work. Do I have a "yes" from you as well, Jazzman?"

"Yes," responded Jazzman. "I will do my best."

"That's what I like to hear," said Dr. Langston as she engaged in sensory communication with both women to gauge their level of responsiveness and willingness to communicate with each other. Years of lost opportunities to mend their relationship based on Colleen's drug addiction and her turning a blind eye to the sexual abuse toward Jazzman.

"I have put together a little homework assignment for you to do with each other outside these sessions, and we will discuss how it has worked out in the next session." Colleen and Jazzman looked at each other in total suspense. Even though one life had given birth to the other, more uncertainty was born in this moment. But Dr. Langston had a relatively simple life assignment for them.

"The assignment will be for you to hang out together and go on a 'mini trip.' I don't care what you do, but just do it together," she explained. "Do you think you can handle that assignment?"

"I think we can," said Colleen nodding her head. Both Colleen and Jazzman seemed to be on board with their homework assignment. But, deep down inside Jazzman was holding onto a dark past—a past created by her mother, which has dimmed her light for years. While an assignment was a great idea, the real homework was trying to understand why her mother never resolved her own life to create a home of love for the two of them.

After their declaration to commit to the assignment, Dr. Langston said to them, "Today, I'm going to give you both a chance to just talk about whatever you want." She then reminded the ladies of the last session when she spoke to them about listening to one another. Dr. Langston wanted them to be active listeners—to listen and be heard—which would benefit their session time. To begin, Jazzman sat in silence while her mother had taken the initiative to speak first.

"Before, pleading for your forgiveness," said Colleen. "I ask that you give your mother a hug," she spoke to her daughter in the third person. This caught Jazzman off guard, but as much as it was a surprise for her mother to want a hug from her, she liked the idea that her mother was showing some compassion and sincerity. This made it hard for Jazzman to reject the sweet gesture.

Both mother and daughter opened their arms to a very loving hug, which was even a surprise to Dr. Langston. "Life hasn't been kind to me," said Colleen. "I've made some choices that I'm not proud of at all," she said while staring into her daughter's eyes, trying to connect to the part of Jazzman's soul that would render the most forgiveness.

Colleen paused and said, "I know that those choices have affected my life and yours in major ways." Again, trying to connect to Jazzman to make her voice be heard and her actions deserving of a second chance.

"I tell people all the time in my drug addiction meetings that your environment doesn't make you who you are," said Colleen, slowly moving back and forth. In this somber of moods, her only goal was to connect with Jazzman. "I grew up in a pretty decent family with both my mother and father. You know this," expressed Colleen. Jazzman shook her head in agreement. She was familiar with her mother's background but didn't know all of the factors that led to her life going astray.

Colleen uttered to Jazzman, "We didn't have it all, but my parents made sure that we grew up in a home filled with love. And I don't blame anybody else but myself for destroying my own life. I have always been rebellious until this day. This confession of emotions was a helpful step in mending their relationship. Colleen's words were heartfelt to a daughter who believed her mother to have abandoned her heart.

"I paid the price in the end for my decision by losing the only daughter I have in this world," said Colleen turning to Jazzman. "I want to be a better person for you, and I am truly sorry for what I did to you. I let my addiction kept me from seeing anything that was going on around me."

Colleen's voice began to tremble as she explained herself to Jazzman. "My self-esteem was low, and every time I tried to do better, my old habits kept pulling me back. I regret missing out on the most important moments in your life. You just don't know how it hurts me every day when I think about everything that has happened and can't go back in time to change a damn thang," said Colleen while wiping her tears with a Kleenex.

"Mama, I understand that you couldn't control yourself," said Jazzman. "But, you knew what was going on with Henry sexually abusing me, and you just sat there and didn't do anything."

There was a deep pain in Jazzman's voice as she spoke. Henry, her mother's boyfriend, had stolen a part of her youth—years of lost life—to never be recovered. "He made me so scared that I thought if I told anyone, he was gonna' do something even more painful like kill you and me. I didn't have a *first time* for sex with someone who I loved because Henry took that away from me," cried Jazzman. Looking toward her mother, she cried out, "Mama, do you hear me loud and clear?"

Louder, she cried out, "Henry took my virginity. He took my innocence. He took the inner joy that every young child should have at that age, and I can't get that back. It's gone!" Jazzman yelled now with her eyelids filled with tears. She had come to learn that a blessed life is not without pain, but she never thought her own mother would contribute to this much pain. Now, both mother and daughter were crying together.

Jazzman had always felt that her mother could have sent her to live with relatives while she was dealing with her addiction. "Mama, I just feel like you could have sent me somewhere else besides being there in that Hellhole," she said, at the same time, searching for the lining of Heaven to guide her words. "I had my daddy, grandma, and grandpa, or even Aunt Tina, but you chose to act like you had it all figured out. I was young, but I knew what was going on," Jazzman told her mother.

She had been waiting for this moment to unload the burden that had weighed her life down. "You would fight with my dad every chance you got whenever he told you that he wanted custody of me. He knew something fishy was going on, but I wouldn't tell him anything when I stayed at his house on the weekends. Even when he'd questioned me about Henry and you, I chose to keep quiet because I didn't want to get you in trouble. But, it was your selfish ways that caused me to keep getting abused by that monster," said Jazzman giving her mother a nasty look.

Silence and tears came over the room as Jazzman poured her heart out to her mother. "Because you didn't want anybody in your business, and I didn't know where to turn, I just got fed up and told my dad," said Jazzman. "I just wanted to get outta' there and for you to get the help you needed."

"Mama, you didn't protect me from that crazy man. It was all about you trying to hide your addiction," said Jazzman. "To make matters worse, when I moved in with my dad, it was hell on a totally different level. It felt like the tale of Cinderella and the wicked stepmother, but with no Prince in the end to take me away. Whenever my dad went to work, his new crazy wife would treat me like crap," Jazzman confessed. "Eventually, I learned to keep quiet and suck it up. I didn't want to make a big deal out of it by telling grandma and Aunt Tina what I was going through because I didn't want them to continue to worry about me."

"You never told me that, Jazzman," said Colleen. "Why would you wait this long to tell me this shit! Excuse my language, Dr. Langston," she exclaimed in disgust, feeling even worse for her absence.

"I am upset right now," said Colleen. "I can't believe that you didn't tell me about that bitch mistreating you."

"And what would you have done?" Jazzman asked this question, knowing that the answer would be unpleasing to her soul. "It was a long time ago, and believe me, that woman is doing everything she can to make up for the way she treated me back in the day."

"Jazzman, if she laid a finger on you, I swear I would…" said a heated Colleen.

"No, mama, she never hit me, ever," Jazzman told her mother. "She took me and her kids shopping and bought them all of the name-brand designer clothes, leaving me with the less expensive clothes. If my dad asked her why I didn't have some of the things he saw her kids wearing, she would make up an excuse of how they didn't have it in my size," said Jazzman. "He was so naïve when it came to that woman."

"Well, Jazzman, you should have said something to your dad about her," said Colleen. It was too late to go back in time, but Colleen wanted to leave that session and go straight to Jazzman's dad's house to give his wife a good beat down. Colleen thought if she could lay hands on that woman, it would make her feel like she'd taken a step forward with mending the broken relationship with her daughter.

"Maybe, I just didn't feel like dealing with anymore conflict," said Jazzman. "I just started to think that was my life. It was supposed to be that way as long as she kept me fed, clothed me, and made sure I had all of the essentials. It was as good as it was gonna' get," Jazzman spoke, reflecting on this time in her life. "My daddy wasn't complaining about her, and I sure wasn't going to say anything."

"Let me ask you a question, Jazzman," said the therapist. "How did this whole experience make you feel?" There was silence in the room. Not a break in the proceedings, but a break in the silence that had held their past lives captured. "With your mother having this drug problem and you then moving in with your father who wasn't at home much to spend time with you?" asked the therapist.

"I just felt alone," Jazzman responded. "I thought nobody really cared about me, so I looked for personal attention in other ways. I needed forms affirmation."

"Now, when you say 'other ways,' what do you mean by that?" asked Dr. Langston, trying to get Jazzman to open up and go deeper into her feelings. Jazzman then hesitated for a moment as she looked downward while fidgeting with her hands before she looked up at the therapist.

"Cutting," she said.

"I started cutting myself," said Jazzman pointing to some of the scars on her arms from the razor cuts. "This one here landed me in the hospital for a few days," pointing to one on her wrist, which had a keloid showing the width of the cut.

"Hmmm," Dr. Langston said, shaking her head as she wrote in her notebook some more. "Was this a suicide attempt?

"I don't know," said Jazzman. "I guess I wanted somebody to notice me hurting."

"After that almost tragic incident, did it open your father's eyes to see that you needed him?" asked the therapist?

"Yes, it did for a while," said Jazzman. "He then took some time off from driving trucks to spend with me. The hospital social worker referred my dad to a psychiatrist for me to see, but that only lasted a short time. My dad's wife thought that the sessions were beginning to cut into her extra allowance money. She then suggested that I quit going because it seemed to her that I was getting better," said Jazzman.

"Did you feel like the therapy was helping any?" asked Dr. Langston.

"Well, I stopped cutting myself, but then I started acting out in sexual ways," Jazzman told her.

"You say 'sexual ways'? Does that mean having multiple sexual partners," added the therapist.

"Yes, my friends and I would hang out with the boys around the neighborhood. I wasn't a virgin, so when the subject came up, I was down for it. By then, I was just trying to fill in the missing void in my life and having sex with all of these different boys gave me the attention that made me feel good. Even if it was for five or ten minutes," said Jazzman.

"Well, Jazzman let me tell you that it is not uncommon for a young woman who has been sexually abused or molested to be very promiscuous in her later years," Dr. Langston confirmed.

"My life just spiraled out of control," said Jazzman.

"Well, I tried to change things when I got off the drugs," Colleen chimed in. "You moved back in with me, and I thought we were making a good connection for a while." Colleen knew her words were difficult to convey with good intentions. She went on, "But, I guess for so long with you doing what you wanted to do listening to me wasn't an option." Suddenly feeling like she needed to defend herself from some of the backlash.

"I admit that you tried to get me back on the right track, but I felt like the damage was already done," replied Jazzman. "I didn't want to listen to what you had to say since you weren't there when I needed you."

"Okay, but shutting me out wasn't gonna' make it better either," replied Colleen.

9

"I know, mama, but I wanted you to hurt just as much as you made me hurt," Jazzman told her.

"I don't understand why you expect me to pay for your problems for the rest of my life," said Colleen, still confused and consumed. "But fine, I got it, Jazz. I admit that I fucked up your life, but you need to finally take some responsibilities for your own actions as well!"

"Alright, let us settle down," said Dr. Langston. She wanted to take back control of the discussion before it got to a point where it would become a screaming match.

"I do take the blame for all the stupid stuff I've done," said Jazzman. "But, if you can admit to your faults with your drug problems, you should also be able to admit that you have replaced one addiction with another one," said Jazzman, loudly calling her mother out.

As the conversation got more heated, Dr. Langston thought she needed to inform the ladies of some office etiquette. "Please try to sustain from using profanity in here," stated Dr. Langston.

"Well, as I was saying…" said Jazzman finishing her thought. "It seems like your drug addiction meetings replaced everything in your life, including me. That's all you ever talked about was your meetings," said Jazzman. "I tried to have a mother and daughter relationship with you, but how could I when it would just turn into a big argument." Jazzman sighed in anger, turning to her mother.

"I surely didn't realize how much I was pushing you away," replied Colleen, disappointed in herself and disappointed in the life she chose.

"After everything that has happened, you should have started at ground zero with your motherly role by first learning how to listen to me," Jazzman advised her. "It was always other things that would take your full attention besides the drug addiction meetings. Like now, this new husband of yours," said Jazzman. "It wasn't even a year ago that you met him and now he is your new distraction.

Colleen was speechless as she sat there, finally keeping her mouth closed long enough to hear what her daughter had to say. Hearing everything that the ladies had to say to one another, Dr. Langston was now ready to make her observation of what she thought about the mother and daughter relationship. She was hoping that she could give the ladies some good pointers on how they could turn things around in their relationship.

Dr. Langston said to Colleen and Jazzman, "A lot was said today, but what I want to happen in this session is for you two ladies to put the past behind you at this moment," she told them, expressing the importance of forgiveness. "Everything that manifested in you before, which causes anger and makes you mad at the other person, needs to be forgiven. Forgive each other and start over. There is no way that the both of you can move forward if you keep harboring over the past. At this point, continuing to be mad at each other will not resolve the problems you have with one another," said the therapist. "Both of you need to try calling each other on a daily basis to establish a friendship first and foremost. You don't have to go in-depth with your personal lives, but at least be cordial with each other. This would be a great way to start."

"Jazzman, you should call your mother more often and ask her how her day went," said Dr. Langston. "I bet that would make her day."

"And Colleen, I want you to just listen when your daughter is talking. You don't have to analyze everything she tells you. Have you ever thought that sometimes people just want a listening ear," noted Dr. Langston. "Do you think that this is something you both can do?" she asked them to be sure that they could accomplish this personal feat.

"Not a problem," said Colleen.

"I guarantee you that taking these small steps will help you to have a healthier relationship," Dr. Langston expressed with a smile on her face and assurance in her heart that the session was productive.

"This session has helped me realize what I was doing was all wrong," said Colleen. She was now starting to see that these sessions were worth the money, time, and mental affirmation she was giving them.

"I have no problem giving my mama a call sometimes," said Jazzman.

"Good, then we are finally making some progress. Please try your best to avoid each other's sensitive spots that you know would cause conflict," said the therapist.

"I guess so," said Colleen giving her daughter a half-smile—half saying, "Yes," I'll try my best—half saying, "I'm still the momma."

"Colleen, be good now," said the therapist concluding the session. Dr. Langston felt a good vibe that the ladies would be back with a new attitude after working to build their relationship. And the homework assignment would definitely help.

Fight For Your Love

THE ARENA WAS jammed packed, and you could hear the bass thumping off of the wall throughout the entire building. B-o-o-m…B-o-o-m…B-o-o-m.

"This concert is off the damn chain," said Roxy. "I can't believe you got us third-row seats. This is the best birthday gift I had ever gotten, baby," she says to Mikayla, trying to speak over the extremely loud noise.

Mikayla dressed in her boyish attire, held on to her woman, who was dressed to impress in an all-red skintight strapless dress and long extensions flowing down her back. The two looked very much in love as they joined in with the loud crowd singing along to all of Mary J. Blige's hit songs.

Don't need no hateration, holleration
In this dancerie
Let's get it percolatin', while you're waiting
So just dance for me

We don't need no haters
We're just trying to love one another

It was now halfway through the concert, and they were still enjoying the sweet songs vibrating through the concert hall. Mikayla sipped on the same beer from her seat the whole night. Meanwhile Roxy had made a friend with the girl sitting next to them who was there with her man. Dancing to the beat, Roxy and her new friend did old dance moves that were appropriate for the limited space they had to work with.

Through the hype of all the excitement, Roxy finally sat down with Mikayla to rest her now hoarse voice. She looked down to pick up her beverage and noticed it was almost empty. "Babe, I'm thirsty," said Roxy. "I'm gonna' run to the concession stand to get another drink. Do you want anything?"

Mikayla replied, "Nah, I'm good." She sat in her seat for almost half an hour listening to the music before she realized that Roxy hadn't come back. Mikayla knew the lines were long, but Roxy was only going to get a drink. "What's taking this girl sooo damn long," Mikayla thought to herself.

It was now intermission, and Roxy still hadn't gotten back, making Mikayla worry even more. She struggled to get through the packed crowd, and what she thought would be a simple task was now becoming more difficult as she looked around in every direction, searching for her girlfriend.

Mikayla ventured to the nearest concession stand to where they were sitting. She scanned the area and then looked over toward the restrooms. Thinking to herself, "The restrooms are right there so where could this girl have possibly gone." She then realized that she was walking around in a circle. "Finally, I found her," thought Mikayla.

"What's taking you so long?" Mikayla said while grabbing who she thought was Roxy from behind by her waist.

"What tha' hell are you doing?" said the unknown young lady.

"Oh…I'm sorry I thought you were someone else from the back," said an embarrassed Mikayla.

"Yeah, you better be sorry," the young lady said with a smirk. She had a look on her face like she wanted to smack the shit out of Mikayla.

"Are you okay, baby?" said the young lady's boyfriend. He walked up and noticed the frown on his girlfriend's face.

"Yeah, I'm alright," she told him. "That bitch over there grabbed my ass thinking I was somebody else."

Mikayla wanted to beat the unknown girl's ass for twisting the story around and calling her a bitch, but instead, she kept her cool, deciding to walk back to her seat. As she walked back to her seat, Mikayla looked to her left thinking that her eyes were deceiving her once again. Her mind had to be playin' tricks on her.

She couldn't believe it was Roxy standing at the entrance of the restroom chatting with another girl who she had never seen before. The two were engaged in a steamy conversation. The girl stood very close to Roxy whispering into her ear, and Roxy was smiling from ear-to-ear, listening to sweet nothings.

"R-o-x-y!" yelled Mikayla. She then walked closer in rage of Roxy's sight.

"Why are you standing here letting this bitch nibble on your ear?" said Mikayla. "You got me running around this damn place looking for your lil' ass, and here you are flirting with this bitch."

"First of all, who are you calling a bitch?" said the freckle face girl nibbling on Roxy's ear. Roxy tried holding back the girl in order to keep the confusion down before it escalated. She didn't want to make a scene noticing that a crowd was beginning to form around them.

"I know yo' fat ass don't want none of this. You will get laid the fuck out messin' with me," said freckle face.

"I doubt it, you freckled face bitch," replied Mikayla. "You couldn't do better, Roxy," said Mikayla. "Trying to cheat on me with this wanna' be hard raggedy Ann looking ass hoe."

"What are you chubby chaser?" said the freckled face girl. Both Mikayla and the freckle-face girl went back and forth, calling each other names.

"Stop it y'all," said Roxy cutting in to stop the altercation. "We are gonna' go to jail," she said, begging them to stop arguing with each other. "Mikayla, let's just go back to our seats. I will explain everything," Roxy told her.

"Nah, I'm about sick of all your explaining," said Mikayla. "You started this shit, and I'm going to finish it." Roxy continued pleading with Mikayla to just leave it alone as she pulled on her arm. "Nah...hold up," Mikayla shouted, pushing Roxy away from her.

"What's up?" Mikayla asked the freckle face girl. "I'll show your ass. I ain't scared."

"Bitch, give yo' brother back his clothes," said the freckle face girl making fun of Mikayla. She then smashed her hand in Mikayla's face as she tried to walk away.

"Nah...hoe, it don't work like that," said Mikayla. She then grabbed hold of the freckle face girl's arm after she smashed her in the face. Tussling back and forth, freckle face girl banged Mikayla upside her head. The catfight was definitely on and poppin' after both women began swinging their fists at each other.

"Let go of my hair," said freckle face girl.

"Nah, you let go of my hair first," said Mikayla.

"Both of you let each other go. Now!" said the tall Caucasian police officer. He had a gang of officers behind him as they shoved through the crowd. "Back up! Back up!" shouted one officer demanding space to assess the situation. He then handcuffed both of the girls and walked them outside to the police car.

"I hope you girls know that you are going downtown tonight," he told them. Mikayla was stoned-faced as she sat on the curb handcuffed.

"Baby, I promised I'll get you out," said Roxy.

"This is your fault. You got me into this shit," replied Mikayla, disappointed in Roxy for putting her in this situation.

***

"Why are you still mad at me?" asked Roxy. "I mean, I got you outta' jail," she told Mikayla.

"Fuckin' right, I'm still mad at you. I had to sit in that cold ass place overnight for some shit that could have been prevented," answered Mikayla. "Why couldn't you have just brought your ass back to your seat like you were supposed to? No, that's too simple. You were at the concert with me. We were having a good time, and you had to go and entertain another bitch."

"Wait one damn minute," said Roxy. "You got your own ass put in jail. Nobody told you to fight that girl. You got a hot temper, and sometimes you need to just chill the fuck out."

"Don't try to spin this, bitch! You are the one who's always putting me in compromising positions to act a fool," stated Mikayla. "I'm really starting to see that you love this shit."

"Love what, Mikayla," said Roxy.

"Don't act dumb, Roxy. You know what the fuck I'm talking about."

The two stared at each other. "You love the drama of making me jealous. I think that deep down inside, you like the fact that you got somebody fighting over your ass," stated Mikayla.

"No, I just think that you are very insecure with our relationship," noted Roxy. "I like that you care so much about me, but sometimes you just jump to conclusions way too fast." Roxy made these comments without acknowledging how she contributed to the drama.

"Well, if I'm so insecure, then tell me what that freckle face bitch was saying to you when I saw her whispering in your ear?" asked Mikayla.

"She invited me to her get out of jail party," replied Roxy. "She even asked me to bring a couple of friends."

Mikayla was beginning to feel stupid for acting all crazy since it was an innocent conversation. "Who the fuck has a get out of jail party?" asked Mikayla looking at Roxy. She still felt like Roxy's story was a little sketchy.

"I'm sorry if my friends aren't college degree nerds like yours are," said Roxy. "Some of us regular folks got to do what we gotta' do to survive in this tough world. If it means doing a little check fraud to get by, then so be it."

"Well, I hope this shit doesn't affect my job now that I have a court date lined up," said Mikayla. She was seriously thinking about how destructive she had become since being in a relationship with Roxy.

"I'm sure everything will be okay," said Roxy. "You were just defending yourself," she told Mikayla.

"In the meantime, your lil' ass don't need to give me anything to worry about from now on," said Mikayla. She was giving her girlfriend one last warning to be caught in what looks like a compromising position.

"Mikayla, girl, I can't do anything about your insecurity. It seems as though you want to control all things in this relationship. It's either your way or no way," stated Roxy.

"If I'm not mistaken, you pressured me to move in with you," expressed Mikayla. "You are the one taking me on this emotional roller coaster ride that I didn't want to go on with you," as she spoke metaphorically.

Mikayla wondered if she could actually deal with Roxy's unpredictable and carefree lifestyle. A lifestyle in which she only valued other people's feelings and emotions after the fact. Both women knew what they wanted from each other, but opposite ways of thinking always caused friction in their relationship.

Homework Assignment

C OLLEEN HAD PLANS to spend a day with her husband Malcolm at the Candle Light Ranch Country Club. Malcolm's brother, Charles, has been a club member for many years and invited them for the day. It was open to extended family and friends on special days throughout the year. Malcolm had managed to get a free day pass from his brother. He and Colleen were going to spend the whole day outside of Houston and enjoy all the amenities of the country club. And most important, they were going to get some much-needed relaxation.

Colleen had been drained with all of her daily duties and was looking forward to the one-day vacation more than anything in the world. After hearing so many good things about the country club, she was thrilled to be able to see it for herself. Malcolm had mentioned the club as being upscale whose members were of elite status. Also, the new resort-style renovations, sounded like a piece of Heaven, and she was delighted to indulge. Colleen couldn't wait to be pampered with a soothing spa treatment.

Her excitement abruptly came to an end. Due to an unexpected workday, Malcolm was forced to cancel, and instead, he suggested that Jazzman go in his place. Even though Colleen wanted to spend some time away with her new husband, she thought it presented the opportunity for the perfect homework assignment for Jazzman and her to do together. This fulfilled the assignment of Dr. Langston to go on a 'mini-trip.'

Colleen thought calling Jazzman on short notice would pose a problem, but to her advantage, she was open to the idea of spending the day out with her mother. Colleen felt that it would give them a chance to bond in ways that they hadn't before. And after an hour and a half of driving and taking in the atmosphere, both Colleen and Jazzman were in awe as they approached the country club. The scenery was breathtaking. The huge gates and beautiful landscape were truly a sight to see as the ladies entered the front entrance of the Candle Light Ranch Country Club. It was everything that Malcolm had described and more. Both of the ladies admired how nice the front entrance looked.

"Wow," said Jazzman. "This place looks more like a mansion than a country club."

"It's beautiful," replied Colleen as they walked into the upscale country club. There was a modern-day southwestern theme, which the women really enjoyed. Both mother and daughter agreed that the country club had all the bells and whistles of how the rich spent their leisure time. Once inside of the club, the ladies stood in the restaurant area, trying their best to blend in before a gorgeous young blonde waitress with a glowing smile greeted them. She then led them to the outside patio, where it overlooked the golf course and a small pond that sat to the side. It was a lovely sunny day to enjoy a wonderful meal outdoors. Both Colleen and Jazzman were ready to take in every bit of the good life.

"Here's a list of fun activities," said the polite waitress. She handed Colleen a piece of paper that gave them a rundown of all the activities easily accessible with the pass. Both mother and daughter didn't complain when they noticed on the paper some of the areas of the club that were off-limits to visitors.

Colleen would have been fine with just a free dinner and spa treatment. Jazzman couldn't take her attention away from the all-American Brad Pitt looking white guys that were walking around like they were members of the elite group.

"Stay in your lane," said Colleen as she noticed her daughter checking out every guy that looked similar to her age group, along with the one black guy who was sitting at the bar by himself.

"What do you mean?" asked Jazzman.

"Girl, you are giving the eye to the one brother in this place," replied Colleen.

"So what, I'm sure he's paid," said Jazzman.

"Yeah, and I'm quite sure he's much older than you, too," Colleen told her daughter.

"Mama, you should know by now that age ain't nothing but a number," retorted Jazzman allowing her eyes to kindly greet the men in her presence.

"Well, I don't approve of you dating somebody that's almost my age. Plus, older men are usually married trying to have a good time on the side with young girls your age," said Colleen in her motherly voice.

"Well, I don't see a ring on his finger," said Jazzman.

"Damn, Jazzman, I didn't know you were looking that hard," stated Colleen. "You just better stay your little ass over here," demanded Colleen.

"Mama, you are so controlling," said Jazzman.

"Damn, right," replied Colleen. "This is mother and daughter time. You can flirt with grown-ass men when you are out with your girlfriends," she spoke bluntly.

"Alright already," said Jazzman trying to keep her cool. "No talking to anybody when I'm with you," she chuckled.

Colleen was unaware of how dismissively she spoke to her daughter throughout lunch. Jazzman wasn't affected at all by her mother's somewhat combative comments, but she took note of it. Jazzman chose to take the high road and let her mother's words go in one ear and out the other. She wasn't in the mood to cause a scene over pettiness when her main concern was to make some progress with their relationship for at least one day. As the evening progressed, Jazzman was happy to get some silence for a change, which was the one thing both she and her mother could agree on.

"Have you had one of these types of massages before?" asked Jazzman.

"No, not quite like this," replied Colleen.

Both ladies laid face down on the massage bed side-by-side wrapped in large white towels relaxing while the well-built men massaged them from head to toe. After the hour-long massage, Colleen was then offered a glass of wine, which she rejected for a virgin margarita along with Jazzman. The ladies sipped on their drinks while enjoying the rest of the evening, concluding with a cucumber and avocado facial along with a manicure and pedicure.

The day had gone better than it had ever before, with both mother and daughter being in the same room together for more than thirty minutes. "Oh my god," said Colleen. "That French-speaking massage therapist, who was massaging me, could definitely come home with me," she said jokingly.

"I don't think your new husband would approve," replied Jazzman with a giggle.

"I'm just playing," said Colleen as both ladies finished the evening with a nice walk outdoors, enjoying the scenery of the beautiful country club. "Oh, look over there," said Colleen pointing in the direction of some bicycles. "Let's take a ride on them," she told her daughter. Colleen started walking in the direction of bicycles.

"I'll pass," said Jazzman.

"Girl, get on the bike and take a stroll down the trail with your mama," demanded Colleen.

"Here, take one," Colleen said, pushing the ten-speed bike toward Jazzman to get on.

"Mama, I said no!" expressed Jazzman.

"Jazzman, what's your problem, girl?" asked Colleen. "You are young and vibrant. Riding a damn bike shouldn't get you that damn mad," said Colleen.

"Mama, I don't know how! That's why!" yelled Jazzman.

"You don't know how?" asked Colleen. "Oh no!" she said, putting her hand over her mouth. "Oh my God, Jazzman… nobody has ever taught you how to ride a bike," she said in tears, disappointed in herself.

"I don't care," replied Jazzman dismissing this void in her life.

"You do care? Yes, you do, Jazzman. The small moments are important, and I wasn't there for the small moments," said Colleen. "It's all my fault that I didn't take the time to show you." At the moment, Colleen wondered why Jazzman's father never taught her how to ride a bicycle. She was again shifting blame instead of accepting blame.

"Let's just leave N-O-W!" said Jazzman. "We've had a good time today, so let's not ruin it with an argument," she told her mother.

"No, we will leave after I show you how to ride this bike," said Colleen. "Let me right my wrongs."

"Mama, please stop embarrassing me out here," said Jazzman as she looked around nervously.

"Jazzman, please let me help you," said Colleen. "All my life, I've screwed up, and this time I have a chance to make it up to you," she said.

"That's fine, but not today, okay," begged Jazzman.

"Jazzman, baby it's all about balance," said Colleen. "It's very easy like driving a car once you focus your mind on it," Colleen said while coaching her daughter.

Jazzman had a feeling that her strong willed mother wasn't going to let this moment pass her by without making her look like a fool in front of all the people that were out there. So, she finally gave in to her mother's attempt to get on the bike. "I can't do this," said Jazzman after she'd tried to peddle and fell off of the bike a few times. "I really don't want to learn how to do this," said Jazzman, now shaking with anxiety.

"Jazzman," said Colleen. "First, you've got to calm down, baby." Colleen said this while giving her daughter a big hug. "Nobody learns how to ride a bicycle on the first try. You can do this," Colleen encouraged her.

Colleen saw the vulnerability written over her daughter's face, which made her want to hold onto Jazzman as if she was an infant baby all over again. Colleen and Jazzman both realized at that moment how much they really needed one another. Colleen then helped Jazzman get back on the bicycle, and the fourth time was a charm. Jazzman found herself peddling all the way down the trail without her mother's assistance.

"Thank you, mama," said Jazzman as she embraced her mother. "You are welcome. Just remember that I always gotcha' back," Colleen told her daughter with a smile. Colleen and Jazzman ended their homework assignment at the Candle Light Ranch Country Club on an excellent note.

Wow!...Impressive Date Night

"UMM...MY FOOD WAS the bomb," said Mia as she'd taken the last bite of her lemon pepper sautéed shrimp. "Expensive," she said to herself while catching a glimpse of the check as Brad signed the receipt.

"I wanted to bring you somewhere nice for our first date," said Brad. "I'm glad that you enjoyed your food because the next one is gonna' be at Pizza Palace," he said with a playful laugh.

"Boy, I like to see you take me to Pizza Palace," said Mia.

"And what Mia...you will be sitting right there with me eating that all-you-can-eat buffet," chuckled Brad.

"Real funny...you are real funny," uttered Mia. She balled up her cloth napkin and threw it at Brad.

Smiling at her, Brad said, "Oh, I see you gonna' do me like this, and I just spent all my money on your dinner."

"Boy, I ain't no dummy, you haven't spent close to all your money from what I can see," said Mia.

"Excuse me, I'm sorry to interrupt your dinner, but could I please get your autograph?" asked the middle-aged white man to Brad.

"Yeah, that's cool," Brad replied to him.

"If you don't mind, could I get you to sign it right here," said the man. He then pointed to the arm sleeve of his Brooks Brothers dress shirt. "I can't believe this," said the middle-aged man. "My son is going to go crazy! You were his favorite basketball player," he told Brad.

"You want me to write it here on your nice dress shirt?" asked Brad. "Yes! Of course, I have about a hundred of these shirts," the man told him.

"Alright," said Brad giving the man what he asked for.

"Thanks again for taken out the time to do this for me. I've followed your entire career ever since your college years at Columbia Tech until the Houston Warriors. It's a shame you had to retire early due to the knee injury. The game could have used you for at least three more years," expressed the man.

"Yeah man, nine years in the game…I think I paid my dues," said Brad reminiscing about his time in the NBA league.

"Well, thanks again, I really appreciated this," said the middle-aged white man.

"No problem, man. I'm always glad to know my fans are still around," added Brad. He then showed the man some love by standing up and extending out his hand to give him a firm handshake.

"Wow! Is it always like this?" asked Mia.

"Sometimes, but since I've been out of the league, the attention various," answered Brad. "Hold on," he gestured, noticing another fan heading toward their table.

"Hi Brad, lately is it?" asked the older black lady.

"Yes, ma'am," replied Brad.

"Well, my husband and I are from Florida, and we are in town to see family. I know I am giving you too much information," said the older lady whose voice began to shake. "But, my husband wanted to know if he could get a picture with you?" while simultaneously pulling the 35 mm camera out of her Louis Vuitton tote bag.

"Sure," stated Brad.

"Okay, thanks," she told Brad. "He didn't know if it was really you or not, which is why he didn't want to come over," said the older lady. "But, I'm not shy like that…you know."

"I hear you, ma'am," said Brad as he looked at Mia with a slight smile. "Tell him to come over." Instead of walking back to her table, the older woman hollered across the restaurant to get his attention.

"C'mon Sammy, it's him!" she said, pointing at Brad while the whole restaurant turned around to see who was shouting. By now, she had embarrassed her husband from the look on his face, but he still walked over to meet and greet with Brad.

"Oh, thanks, man. I told my wife that she didn't need to come over," said the older black man.

"Nah, you're good. I don't mind it at all," stated Brad.

"Got it," the woman said, snapping the picture of Brad standing with her husband. "Now can I get one with you and your beautiful wife?" asked the older black lady. Brad then looked at Mia to see if she was down with being included in the picture. He thought it was cute that the little lady thought Mia was his wife.

"Thank you," said the husband and wife. "Let us leave you two alone and let you get back to your night out," said the older black lady.

"You are welcome," said Brad as he and Mia sat back down at their table.

"Okay, are you ready to leave?" asked Brad.

"Yes, I'm ready whenever you are," Mia replied back.

"If not, I'll be sitting here til' this place closes taken pictures and signing autographs," he told Mia.

"I thought you liked all of that attention," said Mia.

"It's fine, but tonight I don't feel like all that. I'm just trying to spend a quiet evening out with you. Plus, sometimes some of these damn people aren't even fans. They see a crowd and just want to be in it," said Brad. "Could I take you somewhere that's a little more intimate just to talk and hang out?" he asked, sounding like a real gentleman.

"That's cool," said Mia. She was ready to ditch the nice restaurant.

***

Mia found herself in a world that was unlike what she was used to. A V-I-P section at the local club couldn't compare to the very private exclusive lounge she and Brad had just walked into. The lounge was without a doubt a classy place with a contemporary look. It was fit to get a holy nun into the mood for intimacy. The lights were deemed low and the soft sounds of Sade playing in the background. Brad saw the opportunity to move in a little closer to Mia.

> *I gave you all the love I got*
> *I gave you more than I could give*
> *I gave you love*

He scooted himself over to where she had taken a seat on the espresso chocolate-colored rectangular shaped leather couch. He stared directly into her eyes, giving her his full attention.

"Hey there, Mr. Lately, would you like me to open a tab for you tonight?" asked the pretty Spanish waitress.

"Yes, that would be fine," replied Brad. He pointed to Mia to see what drink she would be having.

"I'll take a ginger ale," Mia told the waitress. After Brad ordered his drink, he then dazed into Mia's eyes. Her beauty mesmerized him. Brad was taken back by the glow of her smile.

"You don't drink?" asked Brad.

"No, I don't," she said, veering off topic. "I guess this is where you bring all the ladies, I bet," said Mia trying to size up the situation. She then looked around the high-class establishment at all the model-like beautiful women that were dressed very sophisticatedly. Brad giggled, knowing that the lounge was like the truck stop before the bedroom for many of the athletes and men of his status.

"Ugh…huhn," smiled Brad showing off his pearly white teeth.

"Hmmm," replied Mia with a sigh. She adjusted her short dress to sit like a lady, observing the small crowd that was enjoying themselves at the lounge.

"Did I mention how nice you look in this little black number," said Brad. He had taken his finger and rubbed down the side of Mia's dress.

"No, but thank you," said Mia. "I thought my butt looked too big," she said, fishing for more compliments.

"Girl, your body is banging. You got that curvy pear-shaped body that I like," said Brad. Although Mia didn't need to wear a thousand-dollar dress to look fabulous, she felt there was no way she could compete with these women in the lounge who were flawless from head to toe with their flawless make-up down to their expensive-looking handbags and clutch purses.

See these other women made Mia feel like she was from the back woods of a small town in Texas. Mia thought it was time for her to step up her wardrobe game if Brad was going to continue to bring her to upscale establishments.

"Mia," said Brad. "Are you okay?" he asked. Brad could see that Mia had an uncomfortable look on her face.

"Oh, I'm fine," she answered while in thought. "Now, what were we talking about?" asked Mia.

"Well, to answer your comment from earlier," said Brad. "I've brought a few women here, but that doesn't mean I'm a player. I just like coming here to relax," he explained.

Addressing Mia's question, he added, "I've learned the hard way trying to be a player. Plus, y'all women are too much drama when you get caught. I had to retire my player card," said Brad with a chuckle.

"Have you been hurt before?" he asked Mia.

"Most people have been hurt before, but I just know how men are," said Mia. She thought about all of the bad relationships she'd been in over the years.

"See, I'm not most men," said Brad. "Maybe you just never had a real man in your life. You sound like a woman that has been disappointed, but I could change all of that if you let me," noted Brad.

"Yes, I've had my fair share of crazy relationships, but it seems like all you guys say the same thing when you first meet a girl. Like 'I'm the realist nigga' you ever gonna' meet' and all that shit," said Mia. She had rephrased what Brad said in her own words.

"Even you have admitted to cheating," said Mia.

"Yeah, but every man isn't the same. I do believe that cheaters can change their ways," stated Brad.

"It sounds like you have a story behind your resurrection speech of how cheaters could be reformed," laughed Mia. "You have to show me."

"Well, let me tell you about it," said Brad. He looked down at his Cartier watch before he began telling his story. "You know being a student in college your ass is broke unless your parents had that dough. And nine times out of ten, the black kids I knew got scholarships playing ball or had to take out student loans," Brad explained to Mia. "So, of course, my homeboys, including myself for a while, would talk to these white girls on campus that were into dating black athletes."

"So y'all used white girls?" Mia said in a condensing voice.

"No, they would let us drive their nice ass cars like Mercedes Benz and BMW's, give us money, and take us out to eat, that kind of shit. But, I was starting to feel bad about what I was doing because I knew that I wasn't interested in groupie-type girls," said Brad.

"Plus, I had met one of the few black girls on campus that I was starting to like, but these white groupie girls were persistent, and my third leg kept getting in the way of my good judgment," said Brad. "Well, one of them came up to my apartment that I shared with another teammate and caught me butt-ass naked having sex with the black chick who I had been hooking up with."

"Who let her in?" asked Mia out of curiosity.

"Technically, my dumb-ass roommate," said Brad. "His stupid ass was in his room, playing a video game when he got up to answer the door. Yeah, he had enough sense to tell her that I wasn't there, but his ass was so anxious to get back to the game that he accidentally left the door unlocked. And that crazy white bitch just walked right on in," said Brad remembering that day like it was yesterday.

"There was a lot of arguing back and forth between her and me, then she started talking shit to the black girl. The black girl just left after that. She wasn't entertaining that bullshit," explained Brad.

"All I remember from back then was how she was so damn different from the black chicks I grew up around who would have beat that white girl ass," stated Brad. "But the crazy white girl picked up my small boom box stereo that was sitting on the dresser and threw it at my head. That shit barely missed me. She then trashed my room, like she was going crazy," added Brad. "I swear I wanted to lay her ass out, but I chose to restrain myself from going there with her.

"Nobody told you to put that Mandingo on the white girl. Sounds like you got the ultimate payback," stated Mia.

"Yeah…it was my fault for leading her on when I should have known something was up with that crazy-ass girl whenever she would call me twenty times a day until I answered her calls," said Brad. "Finally, my roommate comes in to see what's going on when he was the cause of the shit," believed Brad. "I had no choice but to grab the bitch by her arms to keep her from breaking my bedroom window. She was about to throw my television set out."

"Did the campus police come to see what was up?" asked Mia.

"Yeah, and her ass filed charges on me trying to say that I slapped her, but it was all dismissed. They couldn't find any physical bruises on her or a witness other than the 'he say she say' testimony. I could have lost my basketball scholarship and everything behind that crazy bitch, so I vowed to only do one woman at a time," said Brad.

"You might want to rephrase that from "do" to "date" one woman at a time," said Mia.

"Well, you know what I mean," said Brad with a boyish laugh. The conversation was very entertaining between the two of them, having their own views regarding relationships. Brad loved the fact that Mia wasn't one of those "Yes" women he usually dated that were too boujee to have an open and honest conversation. They were more interested in his status and how they were going to keep him. Among all things, Mia was a good conversationalist that most men found attractive just as much as her looks. And Mia knew how to use her assets to keep a man like Brad wanting more as they proceeded through the night.

Surprise! Cheese Everywhere

COLLEEN SPECIOUSLY LOOKED around the house as she heard a noise coming from the kitchen. "Hello," she called out, wanting to let whoever was rumbling around in her house know that she was home.

"Colleen, is that you?" asked Malcolm. He walked out of the kitchen with a dish towel in his hand.

"Hi, baby," he said. "Why are you home early?" asked Malcolm.

"The computers went down at work, so they sent us home early," answered Colleen. "What is your reason?" Colleen asked curiously. "I don't recall you informing me that you will be staying home today."

"Well, I unexpectedly decided not to go in today. Working all those long hours at the firm has been stressing me out," stated Malcolm. "I just needed a day off to take a break. Is that a problem with you?" asked Malcolm.

"Oh no," said Colleen. She couldn't believe that her husband had taken off from work to rest, yet he felt the need to clean up the entire house.

"I see the house is spotless," stated Colleen.

"What's wrong with me cleaning?" asked Malcolm.

"Baby, it's not like the house was dirty, but hey, if that's what makes you happy then so be it," said Colleen.

"Guess what?" said Malcolm.

"What?" repeated Colleen.

"I'm making your favorite dish," said Malcolm. "Cheese everywhere," he told her, which meant five different kinds of cheese.

"Um…lasagna," answered Colleen. She had an expression on her face as if she could taste the lasagna just by thinking about it. "What a surprise this is," stated Colleen.

"What do you mean?" asked Malcolm. "A man ain't supposed to clean up and cook for his wife?"

"No, that's not it," said Colleen. "I'm just surprised that you chose to take out the time to treat me like a queen instead of relaxing. I love what you are doing for me!" said Colleen.

"Then sit your hard-working butt down, kick up your feet and relax while I start dinner," Malcolm told his wife. "I even got us a bottle of Merlot. One time won't hurt a thing," stated Malcolm speaking loudly from the kitchen.

"Oh, so you got this whole evening planned out," replied Colleen. She watched her husband from the open den area move around the kitchen with extremely high energy. Colleen thought it was a good time to ask Malcolm a burning question that had been on her mind for some days. "Malcolm, baby, have you seen my wedding ring? You know I only wear it on special occasions," said Colleen.

"Oh shit…I forgot to tell you that I had taken it out of your jewelry box to get it appraised at the jewelry store my buddy works at," noted Malcolm. "He couldn't do it the same day, so I left it with him," said Malcolm. "I'll drop by there on tomorrow to pick it up," he said.

"Baby, why would you take my ring and not tell me?" asked Colleen. "Do you know I looked every damn where for that ring," said Colleen. "I even thought that it must have fallen off my finger at the party we went to last week since it didn't fit well," she said upset.

"Well, you don't have to worry about that anymore either," Malcolm told her. "I got my buddy to size it perfectly for you, too.

"Alright," said Colleen. She felt much better now that she knew where the ring had gone.

"Baby, you will have your ring tomorrow," promised Malcolm.

"Okay, that's fine," said Colleen.

"I wanted you to be surprised since you were always complaining about it being too loose-fitting," said Malcolm.

"Well, thank you, Malcolm. It was very sweet of you to do that," added Colleen. There was an unexpected knock at the door.

"Who is it," Colleen answered the door.

"It's me Jazzman," she hollered from the other side of the front door.

"Jazzman," repeated Colleen with a huge smile on her face as she opened the door for her daughter. "Hey mama," said Jazzman. This was Jazzman's first time seeing their 3500 sq. ft. home.

"What's gotten into you?" asked a shocked Colleen. "What made you want to come see me?" she asked Jazzman. "But, hey, I'm not complaining," Colleen told Jazzman with a look of happiness written over her face.

"I see you made it okay, Jazzman," said Malcolm.

"You called her?" Colleen asked her husband.

"Yes, I did. Remember we talked about inviting her over for dinner," said Malcolm.

"Well, yes," replied Colleen.

"So, I took the initiative to put it together as a surprise for you," said Malcolm. "I called Jazzman up this morning to inform her of what I was going to do for you."

"Wow, Malcolm. I am truly speechless," stated Colleen giving her husband a big sweet kiss on his cheek. While Malcolm finished preparing dinner, it had given the ladies a chance to chat for a bit.

"Well, I was happy when Mr. Malcolm called me about coming over for dinner," said Jazzman. "You know how much I love cheese everywhere," she laughed, remembering when she and her mother first started referring to lasagna as "cheese everywhere."

"Plus, I really enjoyed our time together at the country club, and I thought it would be nice to tell you in person," said Jazzman.

"I enjoyed myself as well," added Colleen. "We should really hang out more often," she said. "I really like how you are putting in the work that Dr. Langston advised us to do. I see a tremendous difference in you," said Colleen.

"I'm glad you've noticed that," stated Jazzman. "So, how's married life going so far?" asked Jazzman.

"Pretty damn good," said Colleen. "What about school?" Colleen returned the question.

"It's fine. I got my first 'A' in my *Fundamentals of Cooking I* class," said Jazzman.

"That's great, Jazz. I'm glad that you like what you are doing with the culinary arts thing," said Colleen, with a smile full of joy.

"I just can't believe how much is involved with cooking and the history of all these different cultures behind it. It's a lot to learn, but I'm interested in learning." Jazzman told her mother.

"I may have you come over to make me and Malcolm a gourmet dish one of these days," said Colleen. Jazzman and her mom sat back on the couch, relaxing until dinner was finally served.

"C'mon ladies," said Malcolm. "It's time to eat," he told them.

"Do you know how to make the lasagna the way my mom and me like it?" asked Jazzman playfully. "Yes, I almost make it better than Tony's Lasagna House," said Malcolm.

"Okay, I will see about that once I taste it," Jazzman said jokingly with Malcolm but serious about her lasagna. Colleen was so delighted to see her husband and daughter getting along like a real loving family.

Hands Down Best Date Ever!!!

MIA SUGGESTED TO Brad that their next date should be somewhere that they could have some fun. All the fancy places with a dress to impress code just weren't Mia's style. She felt more comfortable chilling out on a date that required jeans and a t-shirt. And Mia was feeling good with her Nike cap and sunshades on while riding on the passenger side with the top down of Brad's silver-colored Porsche Boxster.

As Brad drove up to the establishment, Mia recognized the sign that said *Fun Zone*, and she couldn't wait to see what was inside. *Fun Zone* was an entertainment plaza where both kids and adults could enjoy equipped with all the fun amenities set for a fun-filled day. Both Mia and Brad felt like kids again. They were laughing and being competitive with each other as they raced go-karts and played some of the arcade games. Mia hadn't felt this free in a long time, and her sexual tensions were rising high when Brad found ways to get closer to her. The smell of his Dolce & Gabbana cologne hovering over her neck while playing Miniature golf got her juices going. With his very tall, lean body inclined behind her, which naturally made Mia want to poke her butt out a little more, she tried putting the ball in the hole. Miniature golf wasn't Mia's forte, but she didn't mind giving Brad a little something to feel up against his manhood while she acted innocent.

"Look here, Mia," said Brad. "You've got to hold the putter like this," he told her as he positioned her arms to swing the putter in a straight angle. As an athlete, Brad had always taken sports seriously; especially golf, since it was one of his favorite hobbies. "See, there you go. You got it, baby!" said Brad. "Now, keep that stance."

Brad showed Mia exactly how to move her body in order to swing the putter properly on her own. "Girl, I was about to ask if you needed glasses or something," giggled Brad. "If that little girl over there was getting those balls in the hole, I knew you could get just one in," he said playfully.

"Oh, it's like that now," said Mia responding to Brad's dig by giving him a soft shove in his chest. "Maybe her dad brings her out here often to play. Hell, he might be out here grooming her to be the next Tiger Woods, or shall I say, Venus and Serena Williams," stated Mia, assuming the man with the little girl was her father. "But, she's so cute," she said, noticing how the man was taking his time with her.

"I bet you were cute too when you were her age," said Brad taking a glance at the little girl then back to Mia.

"Yeah, I was a little cutie pie," bragged Mia. "But, minus the daddy."

"Well, that makes both of us, because my dad wasn't around either. I don't even know who that nigga' is," added Brad.

"I guess we have one thing in common if nothing else," said Mia. "But, I'm lucky to have my stepfather who has always treated my sister and me like we were his biological daughters."

"Well, that's good to hear," said Brad, bonding with Mia over their daddy issues.

***

"This is the mother fucking life," thought Mia. She was relaxing on a beautiful, sunny, mildly windy day poolside of Brad's Sienna Side Plantation estate in a gated community outside of the Houston area.

"Ms. Harris, may I offer you another frozen lemonade before I leave?" asked the native Mexican housekeeper. Mia had come to like Nina, the housekeeper, after spending almost a week at Brad's home.

"No, I'm fine," answered Mia. "Do you know if Brad called the home phone?" she asked.

"Awww…no," replied Nina. Before Nina could say another word, Brad came walking from the house suited from top to bottom in his golf attire with a cap on, Nike golf shirt, and khaki pants while sporting his white golf shoes. Brad's handsome built body frame looked very enticing to Mia as she looked him up and down the same way she did before he'd left.

"I thought you'd forgotten about me," said Mia.

"I do apologize for leaving you here alone," replied Brad. "But, the guy I had to meet with was my high school coach and mentor," explained Brad. "He helped to get me through some tough times, and now that he's older, whenever he wants me to play a couple holes with him, I feel obligated. You know how that is," he told Mia.

"No, I don't. But, it's all good," said Mia with a smirk on her face. "I'm just kidding," she said. "I can stay here forever and forget about all my damn problems in this big ass house. Do you know that you have entirely too much shit to do at this house? No one would ever need to go outside these gates for anything," said Mia enjoying being in a different atmosphere.

"You are crazy, baby," said Brad.

"No, you are the one that's crazy for having a damn mansion with no one to share it with," stated Mia.

"Have you taken a swim yet?" asked Brad.

"No, I haven't," answered Mia.

"It's also heated if you think it's too breezy out," he said.

"That's not the problem. I don't swim," she said.

"Y'all black women kills me with that saying, 'I don't swim'. Let me guess, it's because it will mess up your hair... right," Brad teased.

"Uh...wrong. Try again," said Mia. "I just don't know how. But, what I do know is how to look very, very and I do mean very sexy in a two-piece swimsuit," Mia said sounding seductive.

"Yeah, you are working that swimsuit," said Brad with a horny look upon his face. "But, I can show you how most people learn," he said, looking as if he was about to do something crazy.

"You bet not!" yelled Mia. "Boy, I swear if you throw me in that pool," she said. Mia then got up from the reclining lawn chair and walked away from the poolside just in case Brad even attempted to throw her in the pool.

"Where are you going, girl? I'm not going to throw you in. Come back," said Brad.

"No, I don't trust you," she said, laughing hysterically.

"Mia...baby come back," Brad promised he wouldn't do it. "Don't be so scary."

"Uhn...uhn," she said with a nervous look on her face.

"Why are you looking like that?" asked Brad. "I'm going back into the house to get out of these sweaty clothes," he told Mia.

"Alright," said Mia, slowly walking back towards Brad. As he walked closer to Mia, she then ran the opposite way, suddenly thinking he was going to throw her in the pool. "Quit running," Brad said. He chased her around the pool.

Then Mia ran into the unlocked Hampton-style decorated pool house. "Come here, girl," said Brad as he finally caught up with her. "Why wouldn't you believe me?" he asked.

CHAPTER 33

"I don't know," Mia told him. "Maybe I still have a phobia from my childhood when my friend's brother threw me in the pool. I almost drowned, and nobody came to my rescue. Like idiots, they thought I was gonna' learn by him throwing me in," Mia explained. "They left me in the pool gasping for my breath until the maintenance man, who worked at the apartment complex where my friend lived, saw me screaming for help, and he jumped in to save me.

"Damn, that's terrible," said Brad. "Well, I'm sorry for playing with you. Can I have a hug?" he asked.

"Sure," said Mia. She let her new man hold her close in his arms to comfort her like a baby. Mia had almost forgotten about the actual baby growing in her belly. She was so happy being with Brad to care about the drama of the last few weeks. And she sure as hell wasn't going to return the missed calls from Claude. As Mia took a quick glimpse into her future with Brad, she was willing to take this secret of her pregnancy with Claude to her grave.

Mia was finally ready to say fuck all that and become the woman she always knew she should be. All she had to do is play the timing right, and she knew she'd get Brad on board with having the baby with her.

Mia had taken Brad by the hand, leading him to the king-size bed in the next room thinking she could use these intimate moments between she and him to solidify her plan to bring them closer together.

"Let's take a shower," Brad whispered in Mia's ear while dibbling on her ear lobe.

"That's even better," said Mia. She then followed his lead into the huge shower, where they both stripped down to nothing. This was like the tenth round of Mia and Brad's sexcapade since she had been staying with him. She was ready for another round of this wild adventure.

"Come here," said Brad. He had taken Mia by the arm as he sat his tall chocolate-built body on the elegant cemented bench in his customized shower. They let the steaming hot water cascade from every angle of the very large showerhead. Mia didn't waste any time straddling Brad in a seated position as the water flowed all over their naked bodies. It felt like they were in a waterfall. Mia was on top of Brad, and he was inside of her. She could feel the wetness dripping all over her body, and he could feel the wetness dripping all over his cock.

The bare lips of Mia's very wet pussy slowly caressed Brad's very long pipe as she moved back and forth with gentle strokes. She then threw her tongue down Brad's throat as they kissed passionately without taking a moment to breathe. The palm of Brad's hand covered Mia's 34D cup feeling the softness of her natural supple breast as each one went into his mouth. He gently licked and sucked all around Mia's now hard light brown nipples, giving each one of them the special attention they deserved. Swirling his very wet tongue in circular motions around the areola of her nipples made Mia want him even more in that moment.

"Damn, you feel so good," said Brad as he held her in his arms. Mia's legs were wrapped tightly around Brad's six-foot seven-inch body frame. Instead of responding to him, she showed him how thrilled she was to be in his presence. Brad effortlessly picked Mia up and carried her to his freshly made king-size bed where they got down to business. She kissed every spot of Brad's hairless ripped, muscular chest, ending up at his very hard package.

Next, Mia chunked a log of spit onto the top of the crown of his twelve-inch erected penis. She had amazing skills, starting from the tip to the shaft to the balls with no hands. Mia went as deep as her mouth would let her, almost reaching the back of her throat. She sucked Brad's cock as if she was working hard for her money. Up and down she stroked it fully with her wet mouth.

Mia then pulled out all of her best tricks in order to give Brad the best lollipop service he ever had. She had her new man howling like a wolf at midnight, as she licked the right spot underneath the crown in circular motions. Mia took her sweet time with every stroke in and around the tip end of his dick while she played with his balls before concentrating on them.

"Oh-h-h shit! Damn, I love the way you suck my dick," whispered Brad. He gently pulled Mia's head up for air. Then he rolled Mia over on her back. She began to purr like a kitten once Brad inserted all twelve inches inside of her moist pussy. Mia was gushing wet. She had already cum while sucking his dick, but now, she was more than ready to explode. In the earlier sexcapades, she had held a lot back. Brad had no idea that she was a squirter, but he was about to find out.

"Fuck me," said Mia. "Fuck me, big daddy," she called him. Mia moaned louder as Brad stroked in and out of her. He loved watching his big cock in her little pussy. His dick fit like a glove to her vagina as he went deeper and deeper into her sea of wetness. He could feel her body clench up and her pussy began to throb slowly, pushing his hard dick out of her. The more he pushed, the more her pussy began to gush. Suddenly, she pushed him all the way out, and her pussy squirted all over his king-size bed.

"Holy shit!" said Brad. In pure excitement, he reinserted himself into Mia to feel the gush of her wetness. Brad was in pure Heaven as he slid in and out of Mia. In the passion of the moment, Brad had cum inside of Mia without even thinking about pulling out. "Oh my God..." he uttered in a state of pleasure.

Girl, Ye-s-s…I Hit Tha' Jack Pot

MIA HADN'T SEEN her best friend, Shannon, since the nightclub outing where she'd met Brad. By now, there was a lot of catching up to do, and Mia thought meeting with her to go shopping would be the perfect outing to fill her in on everything that has happened.

"What's up, bitch!" said Mia jokingly, using the term as a form of endearment. She picked a maternity boutique in the Galleria area to meet with Shannon.

"Hey, girl," replied Shannon. "It's been a minute…huh," said Shannon. "I see a glow on your face," she said with a smile. Shannon was itching to know the juicy details behind Mia's meeting with her.

"What do you mean," said Mia, unable to hold in her happiness.

"Let me guess," stated Shannon. "You met a rich man and got pregnant, or you won the fuckin' lottery," said Shannon. I know it's one or the other, bitch. Spill the tea.

"How did you come up with these two assumptions?" asked Mia laughing at Shannon's presumption.

"Well, you got me in this shop with only maternity clothes. That's a tale-tell sign that you are definitely pregnant. I'm damn sure not," chuckled Shannon. "And girl, you know that I know my designers, and you are surely working that Gucci dress and handbag. Not to mention, those red bottom

Louboutin heels are on point. But, I've never known you to be a label whore."

Shannon knew something was definitely up with her best friend because her wardrobe estimated twice as much as the average person's monthly paycheck.

"Thanks, girl, for the compliment. I have to tell you that your observation is damn near correct," said Mia with a huge smile. "But, really, Shannon," she asked, "Who do you know actually ever won the big lottery?" Both laughed in agreement.

"Hey, anything could happen," stated Shannon.

"You're good at this guessing game," commended Mia.

"C'mon Mia, have you forgotten that I model for a living. And I definitely know top-notch designer's well enough to know that you are rocking the new Gucci bag that I want," said a jealous-looking Shannon. She scoped Mia's hobo handbag inside and out, having already done her research on it. "This damn bag cost about five thousand dollars, girl."

"I know that," replied Mia. "Remind me to give you this bag before we leave here, okay," said Mia.

"Damn, you got it like that now?" asked Shannon. "Okay, give me the details about this rich man who put the bun in your oven."

"Brace yourself because you will never in this life believe what I'm about to tell you," said Mia. Shannon impatiently waited. She was excited to hear one of Mia's long-awaited stories like always.

"Girl, your ass has always got some crazy ass story," said Shannon.

"You will never believe who I hooked up with," said Mia. Who girl?" Shannon asked anxiously.

"Brad Lately," said Mia.

"Who in the hell is Brad Lately?" asked Shannon. "You know the guy I met the night we went clubbing. You know the one who helped me find the necklace that I'd lost on the ground," said Mia thinking her friend would remember him.

"Yeah, I remember him now," said Shannon.

"Well, we have been inseparable," said Mia with a smile on her face that could light up Times Square, NYC.

"Wow!" said Shannon as she looked surprised. "He must have a shit load of money then because your ass is definitely doing the damn thang with it."

"Girl, that motha' fucka' is an ex-ball player. And he is paid," added Mia.

"Come to think of it, I have seen him before at one of those NBA parties," said Shannon.

"Girl, your ass has hit tha' jackpot," stated Shannon. "Plus, you are pregnant by that nigga'," assumed Shannon.

"Hmm…umm," said Mia. "He was in the league for a long time until he suffered a knee injury and had to retire early. "But, now he reports the news for some sports show," Mia told Shannon.

"You mean sports commentator," Shannon said, correcting her friend.

"It's great that you got yourself a league nigga' with some stable money, instead of those damn hustlers that always land their ass in jail," said Shannon.

"Don't try to act like you weren't down with them before you started acting all uppity," stated Mia.

"Whatever, bitch, this conversation is about you, not me," laughed Shannon. She just wanted to hear more details that Mia wasn't quite ready to give truthful answers to. "Now that you are having his baby, should I start picking out a bridesmaid dress soon?" asked Shannon. "Or, is he married already?" she blurted out.

"Hell nah," said Mia.

"Mia, don't play. You know how some of those pro athletes with that type of money have jump-offs on the regular, while their damn wives or main girlfriends be sitting at home with their kids," Shannon said, sounding a little envious by her choice of words.

"I've been staying at this man's house since we went on our second date," stated Mia.

"Damn Mia, your pussy must be made of gold," said Shannon.

"Well, I don't know about all of that," said Mia. "But, once I saw that damn mansion and what he was packing, I knew just what to do to keep that nigga' coming back for more," said Mia giving her girl a high-five.

"You pussy-whipped him," Shannon whispered. Mia then demonstrated with her hands what Brad was packing in the penis department.

"When I was done with him, he didn't want me to leave," said Mia. Shannon was speechless after Mia finished telling her details on how she hooked Brad.

"I guess with the new baby on the way, it's a good thing that he let you move in with him," stated Shannon.

"Well, I haven't gotten rid of my apartment just yet," said Mia. "Actually, I'm finally going home today to check on it."

"It sounds like the sex is awesome, and the money is there for the taken, but do you really like him?" asked Shannon curiously.

"Of course," said Mia. "You saw him with your own eyes. That Brad is fine as hell, plus we had chemistry right off the bat. And I truly believe he's my soul mate," Mia told Shannon.

"Soulmate, bittcchhhh…" screamed Shannon. "Well, it's not often someone comes along like him. Sounds like you have met your prince charming," noted Shannon with a nice smile.

As they walked through the store, Mia began thinking about her pregnancy. "Here, girl," said Shannon handing Mia some maternity clothes she'd picked out. "Now, how far along are you?" she asked. "Because I can barely see a pooch in your belly."

"A little over two months," stated Mia.

"Girl, you are still in your first trimester," replied Shannon. "There's no need for you to be even shopping for maternity clothes yet."

"I thought, why not since I can afford to get them now," said Mia thinking about how she had to bargain shop when she was pregnant with her first two kids. "You know how hard it was when I was pregnant with Jacob and Santana. I couldn't dream of walking into an actual maternity store to buy anything. This week with Brad has been so fuckin' amazing, and I'll be damned if I go back to the struggling life full of hard ache and pain."

"I'm sure Brad is happy about his new bundle of joy," said Shannon.

"He doesn't know yet," said Mia sounding a little hesitant to let Shannon in on her plot.

"Well, you should tell him soon before your belly starts growing," advised Shannon. "If he's the stand-up guy you say he is, there shouldn't be no problems when you tell him," she told her. Mia somehow managed to change the subject and made her way to the register to purchase her clothes. As Shannon and her began walking out of the store, Mia realized that her friend had not gotten a chance to update her on what's new in her life.

"So, what's new with you?" asked Mia.

"Nothing much besides working," replied Shannon. "My agency has been working on getting me this major endorsement with *Love Beauty*," said Shannon.

"The makeup company?" asked Mia.

"Yes, it will be a big deal if it works out," stated Shannon.

"I wish you the best," said Mia. "I love your independence," she told her friend. "You don't need a man for shit. Hold up, I take that back," said Mia. "Except for dick," she said with a chuckle.

"Girl, you are sex-crazed," laughed Shannon. "Yes, I think I have a sex addiction," giggled Mia.

"How's your friend, Tin?" asked Mia remembering the night they all hung out.

"That bitch married a short Asian dude. He's a dentist. They have shacked up, and she quit the modeling industry. Can you believe that shit?" asked Shannon. "She's pregnant, too. All y'all bitches love laying on your back."

"Well, I'll be damn," replied Mia. "She didn't seem like the type of girl to marry a guy like that," said Mia.

"I was shocked, too," added Shannon. "Apparently, she had been keeping him a secret for a long time. I guess fuckin' all those ballplayers and industry niggas was a waste of her time," stated Shannon. "But, it's nice to see she found love in a small package," Shannon said with a little dig. "I wish that I could find true love myself," she admitted. She then looked a little down on herself.

"Don't get yourself down," said Mia. "The right guy will find you in due time."

"I'm just so tired of meeting all of these random, lame-ass dudes who just wanna' hoe around and be dishonest," said Shannon.

"You are a smart, beautiful model, and one of these days, a man will come around with all the qualities that you want," said Mia giving her friend a big hug. "And he will rock your world!" added Mia with a chuckle.

"Well, maybe I could let go of a few petty must-haves on my list," said Shannon. Both Mia and Shannon enjoyed their girl's day out and vowed to keep in touch on a more consistent basis. Even with Shannon's conservative ways, Mia knew her friend wouldn't critically judge her crazy life.

Feening For a Hit…

MALCOLM'S ALTER EGO had completely taken over him. He was parked alongside of a rundown convenient store in the roughest neighborhood he could find. "Say Youngblood," he called out to the young-twenty-something-looking guy who was hanging out in front of the store. "Come over here and let me holla' at cha' for a second. I got some stuff I'm trying to get off my hands," he told him. Malcolm popped open the trunk of his Ford Expedition.

"What you got?" asked the guy. He had focused his attention on what Malcolm was selling.

"Look here, man, I got a bunch of women's clothes. They're all in a size six. Do you wanna' buy some of this shit? I know you gotta' girlfriend who could wear this shit," said Malcolm.

"Nah, man, I'm good," stated the young guy after suddenly being uninterested in what Malcolm was selling.

"C'mon, man. See, this is some real quality designer shit, just take a look," he begged him. "You tell me you don't know anybody that can use a Donna Karen dress or these brand new Coach shoes. I didn't know these were back here, my damn self," said Malcolm noticing a Saks 5th Avenue outlet bag in the trunk that his wife must have gone shopping and forgot to take it out. "Now we talking," stated Malcolm as he rumbled through the bag feverish in search of making this deal worth the young guy's time. "Look here, man," said Malcolm. "What can I get for a brand new Prada bag, shoes, and this bottle of Versace women's perfume, plus I'll throw in the rest of these designer clothes," he said using the worst negotiation skills ever.

"Hmm… I don't know," said the young guy. He was hesitating to purchase Malcolm's items.

"Fifty dollars and all this shit can be yours," said Malcolm. He was anxious to get his stuff sold. "Okay, thirty-five dollars, you can't beat this, Youngblood. I got Coach, Donna Karen, and Nicole Miller. This shit cost money." Malcolm went down the list naming all of his items. "Ask any woman who knows about fashion, and they will tell you this stuff ain't cheap," said Malcolm getting a little frustrated.

"Well, my mama's birthday is coming up soon," said the young guy.

"Alright then," stated Malcolm. He was becoming more anxious by the minute.

"I got you," said the young guy checking out his surroundings before making the transaction. "Why don't I just give you this as a trade-off," he said, seeing how bad Malcolm appeared to be feening.

The young guy had given Malcolm a crack rock he thought would be enough to pay him for all the stuff he was getting, but there was clearly a misunderstanding. "Damn, youngster, you can't give a brother more than this little shit?" asked Malcolm. "I know you gonna' probably sell some of this shit and make a real profit."

"Hold up," said the young guy. "I'm helping yo' ass out, so you either take or leave it. Better yet, get tha' fuck outta' here cuz' this is my territory right here," said the young guy. "You're messing up my hustle trying to sell this shit on my corner."

The young guy turned into the typical D-Boy stereotype with a short temper. "As a matter of fact, give me all this shit and get the fuck outta' here," he told Malcolm. "And, if I ever see yo' ass around here again, standing on this corner, yo' ass gotta' another thing coming to you," said the young guy. He then raised his white T-shirt and pointed to the 45 Smith and Wesson he was holding in his pants.

"Youngblood, I don't need no trouble," stated a very scared Malcolm.

"Well, get in that motha' fucking truck and get the fuck outta' here then," said the young guy. Malcolm couldn't close his trunk fast enough from feeling a fist going upside his head as he turned to walk to the driver's side of his truck.

"What was that for?" asked Malcolm.

"You ain't moving fast enough old man," said the young guy. He pushed Malcolm in the back of his head some more to get him to move along faster. "I got a customer who needs this spot, and yo' ass is taking up space."

"Alright, you ain't gotta' be so violent," said Malcolm.

"Shut tha' fuck up," the young guy told him as he gave Malcolm's truck a swift kick in the front end. Malcolm jumped into his SUV truck, like a flash of lightning, and pulled out of the tight spot burning rubber as he sped off.

Unwanted Misery

"N-O-O-O," SCREAMED COLLEEN. "Somebody, please tell me what the hell is going on!?" she shouted and asked at the same time. Colleen was shocked after scrambling through all the junk mail and came across a past due notice sent from the mortgage company. *We regret to inform you that you are two months past due on your mortgage payment.* She continued to read the letter out loud.

Colleen couldn't believe what she had just read. "Oh no, this must be an error." She did a quick review in her head. Colleen immediately picked up the phone to call her husband, letting the phone ring several times before hanging up. Colleen needed to vent, and she knew that she could call on her sister Tina for some sound advice in situations like this one.

"Tina, girl!" she shouted over the phone.

"Hello, Colleen is that you?" answered James.

"Yeah, it's me," she said. "Is Tina there?"

"She's in the other room," James told her. "Tina, baby, your sister is on the line," said James. "So, how's married life been treating you?" asked James.

"It's going alright," Colleen replied back. "It's funny how you find out new things about your spouse after you've tied the knot," she told James.

"Well, that's what dating is for," said James. "It's easy to get in but hard to get out," he told her. James could tell in

Colleen's tone of voice that her newlywed stage wasn't going as planned, but he wasn't going to be the one to address her issues.

"Honey, I got it!" Tina yelled out.

"Girl, I'm mad as hell," stated Colleen.

"Mad at what," repeated Tina. "You just got married, bought a big new house, and things are going good with you and Jazzman. What can possibly go wrong now?" asked Tina.

"Malcolm has been acting very strange lately," replied Colleen.

"I bet he's on that stuff again," Tina had taken a lucky but correct guess.

"Well, I'm not for sure if that's the case," stated Colleen. "I didn't want to tell anyone that I put up all of my savings on the down payment for the house," Colleen began to tear up. "And in return, Malcolm was supposed to pay the mortgage from then on. But, I just came across a two-months past due mortgage notice," said Colleen.

"This motha' fucka' hasn't paid the mortgage for two months!" Colleen yelled through the phone. "Now, you tell me why he hasn't made not one damn payment since we moved in."

Angrily, Colleen went on, "I'm about to be three months behind now that the new payment is approaching the deadline." Tina did not know how to handle her sister's problem because she had her own issues that she was dealing with at the time. Colleen had always come to her for advice, and being the big sister that she was, Tina felt it was her responsibility to talk with her sister.

"Have you talked to him about this yet?" asked Tina. "No, I haven't. I tried to call him, but he hasn't picked up his phone all day," said Colleen. "Plus, he took my wedding ring without my knowledge, claiming to have taken it to get it appraised," stated Colleen.

"Damn, Colleen, I hate that you got conned by that crack addict. If what you are saying is true, then it is definitely a possibility that he's back on drugs," noted Tina.

"Believe me, I know how a drug addict looks and acts," said Colleen. "All the excuses he'd made about the wedding ring and his hyper actions lately are all signs of a crack head. I just wonder what his excuse will be once I talk to him," stated Colleen.

"First, you need to check your bank accounts," said Tina.

"Thank God we didn't join our accounts like we were going to do," stated Colleen.

"Well, good," said Tina sounding relieved. "Do you have access to his accounts?" asked Tina.

"Yes, but I'm not the type of woman that snoops around in my man's business," said Colleen.

"You are married to the man," noted Tina. "You have a right to snoop around in your man's business," stated Tina. "That's how marriage works, especially in this case when bills aren't getting paid on time, then it's definitely fair game," she told Colleen. "Check his accounts," strongly advised Tina.

"Okay, I will do it," Colleen said with a sigh. "Colleen was having a hard time believing her husband was back on drugs after all they've talked about. She would have never thought he'd relapse. It hurt her just thinking about all the time invested in him.

"Maybe he's just absent-minded," said Colleen making excuses for Malcolm. "You know how men can be very forgetful." Colleen was starting to think it was her fault for not attending to the mortgage. She began to fully blame herself.

"I know you want to believe the charming man that you married isn't back on drugs, but you need to get out of denial. I would hate for you to come home one day to find out he has sold all your shit for a ten-dollar crack rock," stated Tina. "I told your ass that you were jumping into marriage way too fast," Tina told her sister.

Although the truth was beginning to unfold, Colleen wanted to forget about everything that was happening to her. She almost wished she could continue to be blinded by Malcolm's strange behavior, but knowing all too well on how the addiction could turn you into your worst enemy, Colleen had to do something soon.

"Maybe, I should talk to him first about his actions," said Colleen.

"Did I hear you correctly," responded Tina. "Either he's on that dope or not," said Tina. "I don't have time for this shit. You asked me what to do, and I'm telling you to leave him before things go from bad to worse," stated Tina. "Now, it's up to you to figure out how you are going to handle this problem."

"Well, I'm going to be fair and give him a chance to tell his side of the story before I jump to conclusions," said Colleen.

"Looks like you got it all figured out," said Tina. "Now, I'm going to leave you to your fantasy of thinking Malcolm just needs a little fine tuning," said Tina before slamming the phone down in Colleen's ear.

Although Colleen was distraught with her sister, she understood that the real problem was with Malcolm for putting her through all of this unwanted misery. Colleen couldn't understand how God could send her everything she wanted in the palm of her hands just to take it away in the blink of an eye. She was disappointed and confused with all the craziness in her life, which drove her to finish the bottle of Merlot she had leftover on the wet bar.

The Ultimate Price to Pay

"Where tha' hell have you been?" asked Colleen to Malcolm. There was no denying that Malcolm looked as if he'd been wearing the same clothes for an entire week, and his explanation was about as weak as a sick puppy on his last two legs.

"Your ass left here last week to go to work," she said. "P-l-e-a-s-e get the hell out of my face!" stated Colleen.

"Baby, don't do me like this," begged Malcolm. He then reached out his hands for his wife's forgiveness.

"Don't you touch me," Colleen said, pulling back from him as he proceeded to come closer.

"What happened to the vows we took 'for better or for worse?" asked Malcolm.

"Those vows were bullshit because you have been lying to me since day one. Please tell me how we can build love on a foundation of lies?" replied Colleen.

"I haven't lied to you," said Malcolm with a dumb look on his face.

"Don't make me..." Colleen said to herself. "I'm just going to put it out there," she said. Colleen was fed up with Malcolm's ridiculous act.

"Where's my wedding ring, Malcolm? What happened to you picking it up from your buddy's jewelry shop?" she asked him. Colleen didn't wait for an answer as she continued to hit Malcolm with more of his lies. "And this would be lie number two," she said. Colleen slammed the mortgage foreclosure letter down on the coffee table. "Read it, she demanded to Malcolm. Colleen stared at her husband as he scanned over the letter. Malcolm had realized that all of his lies had finally caught up with him, and there was nothing he could say or do to soften the pain he had caused his wife.

"Colleen, baby, what had happened was," Malcolm stumbled through his words.

"Stop with the fucking lies," said Colleen. "You haven't paid one single payment on this fucking house since we have been living here," she said, shaking her head. "Malcolm, you have disappointed me in every way," said Colleen. "Have you looked at yourself in the mirror lately," she said. Colleen could hardly stand close to her husband as she snared up her nose from the smell that reeked of a dirty stinky odor. "You had me believing what we've had was real, but all along, you played me," said Colleen. "Taking my kindness for weakness was a low-down dirty thing to do."

"Colleen, don't be such a drama queen," said Malcolm. "You are making this out to be more than what it is," he told her. "I will pay the damn mortgage payment today if that will make you happy," he told Colleen.

"Drama queen! I dare you! Malcolm, you are a sick individual," said Colleen. "Where are you going to get the money?" she asked. Then, she slammed his bank statements on the coffee table, showing proof of all his empty accounts with over-drafted charges. "You have no money unless you have some cash stashed somewhere in a hiding place," stated Colleen.

"That's my personal stuff you are messing with," stated Malcolm.

"Well, you should have found a more secure spot to hide your stuff instead of a shoebox at the top of the closet," added Colleen.

"How about you show me your bank account statements," he told Colleen. She realized their privacy was what got them into the mess they were in in the first place. She wasn't about to give her husband any more authority than he had to mess up her life even anymore.

Colleen noticed a trend in Malcolm's bank statements that showed his bi-weekly paycheck being directly deposited and withdrawn on the same day. That went on for a couple of months. She had pieced together the missing puzzle noticing there wasn't any money directly deposited in the last few weeks.

"What's going on with you, Malcolm?" asked Colleen. Malcolm was speechless and incapable of answering his wife's questions.

"Damn it, Colleen. I don't know what to tell you," responded Malcolm. Malcolm rubbed his head like it was too much for him to deal with. "Fuck this house," he said, surprising Colleen with his profanity.

"Fuck this house, huh? Well, I'm glad you said that. Your bags are already packed," stated Colleen.

"You did what!" Malcolm exclaimed.

"I didn't stutter," said Colleen. "You got to go," she said, pointing toward the garage door. "Call me later, and I will send the rest of your things then," Colleen told her husband.

"I can't believe you are putting me out of my own damn house," said Malcolm. He was very much shocked by Colleen's actions. "We bought this house together. I'm not going anywhere until we settle this," stated Malcolm.

"There is nothing to settle. It's clear to me now that you weren't going to ever change. I be damned, if I put myself in a defenseless state ever again," said Colleen. Malcolm was unaware that the consequences would cost him the ultimate price to pay.

"I left to clear my head of some stuff and look what happens!" Malcolm blurted. Malcolm felt like his wife should have warned him that she would run off when times got a little rough.

"Well, you should have come to me like a real man instead of running away. I would have been there for you if you would have let me in," stated Colleen near tears. "My sister was right about you, but I was just too blind to see it. I jumped into this relationship way too fast," she said.

"Are you saying that you regret marrying me?" asked Malcolm.

"Well, if the shoe fits," answered Colleen.

"Colleen, your ass was just a gold digger. You weren't saying a thing when I was taking you to all of those fancy restaurants," said Malcolm. "You used my credit cards to buy all of your designer outfits," he told her.

"In the end, it cost me more money than what you could have ever spent on me," noted Colleen.

"I can't believe you told your sister my business," said Malcolm.

"Well, it's not a secret that we met in a drug and alcohol addiction meeting," said Colleen. "And I refuse to compete with your drug habit, so it's best that we end this marriage now," she told him.

"You don't know what you are talking about," said Malcolm. He trembled as if he needed a fix.

"Malcolm, your ass is feening now," replied Colleen. "And I can't give you the help that you need," she said. "You sold my clothes for dope."

"M-a-n...Colleen, that damn cleaners burnt down," he told her. Colleen looked at Malcolm with a peculiar smile on her face. She finally recognized that her husband was a pathological liar and on top of that a crack head who couldn't kick his addiction.

"I should thank your brother for filling me in on everything," said Colleen.

"My brother," said a furious Malcolm. "I can't believe you called my brother. What tha' hell were you thinking?"

"How else would I've been able to conclude my assumptions," said Colleen.

"You are a natural-born bitch," said Malcolm.

"Your brother, Charles, told me everything about your bipolar ass who can't handle the slightest pressure," said Colleen. "Plus, he let me borrow the money to pay the mortgage that your ass fucked off."

"Did he also tell you that he fired me in order to hire a twenty-something-white-ass-whore that he's been messing around with behind his wife's back?" asked Malcolm.

"Well, it's two sides to every story and right now your side isn't credible," said Colleen.

"Just keep on believing every damn thing people tell you instead of your own husband," said Malcolm. "So I guess Charles was lying about you being unreliable and that he can't depend on you to be on time to work or let alone come to work?" Colleen questioned him. "He's just as tired of your shit as I am."

"Well, can I at least use the phone to call a taxi?" asked Malcolm. "Where's your mobile phone?" said Colleen.

"I lost it, okay," replied Malcolm. Colleen had taken a peek out of the window and saw that Malcolm's SUV truck was nowhere in sight.

"Let me guess, you lost the truck, too," stated Colleen. "Nah, you let a buddy use it. I bet you lent it out to a drug dealer for ten dollars," she said.

"Actually, it was twenty dollars, to be correct." Colleen was disgusted with Malcolm, but she still found it in her heart to reach into her purse to give him fifty dollars.

"Please be safe," said Colleen.

"You don't have to worry about me. I will be just fine," said Malcolm.

"All I ask of you is that you find what's missing in your life, which keeps you going back to your demons," Colleen said as a farewell goodbye. She found it hard to shut out the man she had grown to love out of her life forever.

Mystery Man

THERE WAS ROXY, waiting for her mystery man to arrive. She waited for him in the Four Seasons hotel's presidential suite. Roxy wasn't truthful with her sexuality. She was bi-sexual, but a lot of people didn't know it. Deep down inside, she found true love for the one and only man she had loved for a long time. Roxy seemed to have a carefree spirit, which she used as a defense mechanism to hide her true feelings. And now that her relationship with Mikayla was on the rocks, it was long overdue for her to express how much she truly loved her mystery man.

"Hey, baby. What took you so long?" asked Roxy as she sat on the fluffy king-size bed with the lights pitched black.

"Well, I'm here now," replied the tall, dark, handsome man. "You know your way around this place," he told her. Roxy didn't want to cause any drama, even though she knew it wasn't in his character to have her waiting. As soon as the mystery man turned up the adjustable light switch, he could definitely see why Roxy questioned his late arrival. She was dressed to kill in her bright red pan leather thong suit with the matching police-style hat, ruby red lipstick, and nail polish to turn her man on.

The mystery man walked over to the five-foot three-inch beauty where he stood in front of her looking like he was about as tall as the Eiffel tower standing up against her; even with the six-inch stiletto heels on, she barely came close to his armpits. "Hmmm…I see you went all out," he said, grabbing her butt cheeks. He rubbed on it with the palm of his big hands, then smacked her backside just to see how firm it still was. The mystery man wondered what was up with the costume Roxy was wearing, but his main concern was how he was going to get her out of it.

"Awww…pan leather," he said while moving his hands up and down her thighs. "And fishnet stockings," he added. "Role-playing?" he asked with laughter.

"I told you over the phone that tonight was gonna' be special. I thought that maybe you've gotten bored, which is why you hadn't called me in a while," Roxy told him. "Am I not good enough for you anymore?" she asked. Roxy looked up to the tall, gorgeous man while she reached down into his pants to feel his manhood.

"I guess you can say that some things have changed," stated the mystery man. "It has nothing to do with you. I've been very busy lately," he told her.

"Just relax and let me take control," said Roxy. She dimmed the lights to set the mood.

"Damn, you are sexy," said the mystery man as he ran his hands through her silky straight twenty-inch long jet black locs. "Hold up," said the mystery man. "Are you trying to handcuff me?" he asked Roxy.

"Well, yeah," answered Roxy. "It's all a part of the role play," she told him.

"Man…Roxy this is crazy," he stated. She was starting to feel foolish for trying to keep their time together fresh. "I can see that you went out of your way to make this night special," said the mystery man. "But, the handcuffs isn't what I'm into," he told her.

"Well, I guess the whip is a no-no, too?" asked Roxy.

"Unfortunately, I'm not into whips either," he told her. He thought Roxy was out of her mind to think he would let her hit him with a whip. He wasn't the type of man who was into the freaky dominatrix kind of sex. "Do you accept my apology?" he asked. "Yes, no, or maybe so," he said, waiting for her to respond.

"We are cool," she said, playfully, pushing him off of her. "I should have called to let you know that I was stuck in traffic," he acknowledged. "I've been working on some big investments to secure my early retirement," said the mystery man.

"Nigga please, you are already paid," said Roxy. "Boy, I swear niggas are never satisfied."

"Baby girl, you know when a nigga' got expensive taste, it comes at a cost," he replied. "Plus, I fucked off a lot of money in my younger days, and now it's time that I make major moves to keep my legacy going strong, money and all," noted the mystery man.

"Well, it ain't nothing wrong with that," Roxy agreed with him. "I've missed you so much," she said.

"Same here," said the handsome man. He then slipped Roxy a wet kiss using the tip of his tongue and moving it down to her neck. Roxy started off the night of passion with one of her lap dances that she was famous for at work.

She began by playing her favorite R&B group, Jodeci.

Lady, I'm hooked on you,
There's nothing else I'd rather do,
spend my last dime for a drop of your time...

The mystery man sat on the king-size bed and watched as the beauty worked her magic. Slowly pushing her ass on top of his very hard genitals, Roxy moved in a sexual gyrating circular motion—moving up and moving down and moving all around—feeling what she had been missing for such a long time. Her clothing came off with every classic erotic move she made.

"Do you like it, baby?" she asked him.

"I love it, girl," said the mystery man. "Keep popping that ass on me just like that," he said. He helped to pull down her pan leather thong and fishnet pantyhose down to her ankles. After her very sexy lap dance, she was left with only her bustier on. Roxy then faced forward, straddling her smooth chocolate thighs around his waist as she sat on his lap to give him something to feel. Soon the top was off, and the mystery man and Roxy were engaged in a hot steamy position.

As their bare bodies rubbed together horizontally, the tall, dark handsome man made up for his tardiness as he gently rubbed his big hands all over Roxy's supple nipples. Her breasts were perfect—round and soft with erect nipples. He then licked them thoroughly until they became harder with every stroke of his tongue. The mystery man began to make his way down to her pussy where he then fingered her until she was soaking wet. One inch in, and then he curled his finger to find her G-spot. In chorus, he used his tongue to massage Roxy's clit until she began to sing a sweet melody. She was amazed by what a tongue was capable of doing as she moaned and groaned feeling every nook and cranny of her pussy being eaten in ways she never even imagined.

"Oh-h-h-h…baby, you sure know how to lick the clit," she whispered while pushing his head further inside of her vagina.

"Just lay back and let big daddy cum inside," he said as he put his manhood inside of Roxy.

"Go deep, baby," said Roxy with her legs held mid-way in the air. The man of her dreams was now in full flesh and making her body feel really good. Roxy loved to talk dirty as he put it down on her. "Work that big dick inside of me. I can take it, baby!" she screamed loudly.

"I know you can," replied the handsome mystery man.

"Uh..uh…damn girl, I almost forgot how much I missed you until now," he said in the heat of passion with sweat dripping all over her body. She then switched positions and hopped on top of her lover's huge dick like she was riding the winning horse in the Kentucky Derby.

"Oh-h-h shit," said the mystery man.

He moaned continuously from the amazing loving Roxy was putting down on him. She hopped up and down on top of his Johnston like she was on a pogo stick. Roxy spanned around while his penis was still inside of her, ending up in the same direction with her ass in his face while she pounced on his dick as if she was saddled up on a horse. Roxy handled every inch of his dick with endurance until he came inside of her. "Damn, your ass knows how to put a nigga to sleep, don't you," he told Roxy.

"Well, I aim to please," stated Roxy. Both the mystery man and Roxy laid in the bed tired and sweaty from the great sex they had just taken part in. Roxy wished she could have this feeling every day because the homey-lover-friend relationship was getting old to her. It was time that her mystery man knew that she wanted a traditional relationship that consisted of commitment, love, respect, and maybe even a family one-day. She never knew what a family dynamic was like, but she wanted to find out but only with him. Roxy pictured it all in her head that she would have two boys and one girl whom they would call 'Princess', because her father would treat her as if she was one.

Roxy liked the idea of a man being a man and working to provide for his family while the woman stayed at home to take care of the kids. She couldn't understand why so many women thought being submissive to their man was wrong when she felt it would be nice to let a man think he's in control without being over-aggressive. But, through so many failed relationships with men taking advantage of her, she soon stopped thinking about being with the man of her dreams.

So, she began her quest to be with the same sex because women understood her emotionally and physically. Although her mystery man couldn't commit to her, nor did he love her the way she wanted to be loved, he'd shown her a level of mutual respect that kept her intrigued by him. Besides his charming personality and good looks, he was a man she could see a future with if only he knew how much she would kill to be with him.

"Do you really know how special you are to me?" asked the mystery man. He covered his soft lips over Roxy's lips, gently giving her a taste of his tongue once again to last until the next time they saw each other.

"Tell me something 'B'," she called him by his nickname as the two of them laid across the bed. They were relaxed and passed a joint back and forth to one another. "We have a connection, but why haven't you made our relationship official?" she asked him. Roxy blew out the smoke like she was a pro at it. "We both have had a fucked up childhood but managed to get through it. We both love money, life and fucking. But aside from that, we genuinely like the same movies, goofy shit…everything basically," stated Roxy. "What's wrong with me?" she asked.

"It's nothing wrong with you," answered B.

"Well, I'm tired of you playing the boyfriend role when it's convenient for you?" said Roxy. She thought the circumstances of how they met might have caused a conflict due to the fact that she wasn't the girl next door. But, as time passed, 'B' got to know the real Roxy for more than just taking off her clothes, she was as sweet as pie with a big heart.

"Man…Roxy, do you really wanna' bring this up now?" asked 'B'. He then passed the joint back to Roxy.

"Don't you think I have a right to know why you can't be with me?" she questioned him.

"I would rather have you as my very best friend than to ever lose you behind a bad break-up," he told her. Roxy giggled from what she'd just heard, and 'B' almost choked his self to death from laughing so hard. Both Roxy and 'B' couldn't stop themselves from the meaningless laughter.

"That sounds like a hallmark card that somebody would send yo' ass when they don't know how to let you down face-to-face," stated Roxy.

"I was going somewhere with this before yo' ass started laughing," he told her.

"Okay, I'm listening," said Roxy, still laughing from the effects of the joint.

"I would hate to get into a relationship with you, and it doesn't work out," stated 'B.' "You've been through a lot, and I would hate to break your heart. Plus, we have a special friendship that I want to cherish," added 'B'. "You know how y'all women are when the relationship goes bad," stated 'B' as he gave her a kiss on the forehead. "You and your little girlfriends would be stalking me, keying my cars, and breaking out the windows."

"I'm not that type of girl," Roxy told him. Roxy looked like the young and naïve girl who went along with her mystery man's decision to just be friends.

"But, who's to say you will be the one to break my heart," stated Roxy. "Honestly, we would never know," she said, dazing into his eyes. All along, 'B' wondered if he was passing up a chance to be with the right woman.

Another woman was also occupying his attention, and he had to first see where their relationship was going before he could take Roxy up on her offer. It was easier for him to keep Roxy on the back burner while he figured out his options. "You aren't ready for all of this chocolate love," said Roxy with a chuckle. "I bet you are still running after all those light-skinned hoe's that's got your ass on a wild goose chase," she said, reading his mind.

"What you talkin' about?" said 'B.'

"I'm not stupid, you know," said Roxy. "All the pillow talks we've had, it's like those types of women are the only ones who could get you to commit," she stated.

"Let's get something to eat because I'm hungry as fuck," Roxy suggested. 'B,' the mystery man was starting to think that maybe he did have some self-hatred harboring inside of him, which led him to fall head over heels in love with women of a lighter-skinned complexion. Meanwhile, Roxy wondered if she had enough love for 'B' to continue on with their homey-lover-friend relationship.

H-E-L-P! Crazy on Tha' Loose

AFTER BEING BACK home at her apartment, reality had set in. Mia stared at the four corners of the walls in her bedroom, wrecking her brain at the thought of having to tell Brad her dilemma. She struggled with the idea of maybe losing the man she had come to love in the process. In the few days she'd spent at home, Mia's nerves wouldn't allow her to eat or sleep, as she rationalized the reasons she should have an abortion.

Mia became depressed to the extent of unplugging her phone to distant herself from everyone, including Brad. She sat in bed with her eyes filled with tears avoiding all of Claude's calls. Mia suddenly realized that she needed to quit drowning in her tears and make a decision based on her own terms. After Mia saw her reflection in the bathroom mirror, which showed a very pale face and naturally curly wild hair, she had to come up with an airtight plan that would relieve her from all of her problems. Mia prayed that Brad would accept her pregnancy with an open heart when she tells him that he will be a father soon. Although Mia's stomach turned inside and out just thinking about her dishonesty, it was the only way to secure her future income and get crazy Claude off her back as well.

***

Knock...knock...

"Who could be knocking on my door this early in the morning," wondered Mia as she struggled to get out of bed. She couldn't see clearly through her peephole, which made Mia reluctant to open the door. "Who's there," Mia yelled.

"Your neighbor, Alexis," replied the little girl. Mia then felt compelled to open the door to see what the little girl wanted.

"Hi, ma'am," said the little girl. "I'm selling some girl scout cookies. Would you like to buy a box?" she asked. The little girl showed Mia all the different types of cookies she had in her bag.

"How much are you selling them for?"

"Five dollars," answered the little girl. "Everybody usually buys two boxes because they are the best cookies in the world," she told Mia smiling from ear-to-ear.

"Well, aren't you the most persuasive little salesperson I'd ever met," Mia replied with a smile back. "You just hold on, and I will be right back with the money."

She then ran to her bedroom to get some money.

Upon her return, "Claude!" she exclaimed. "Where is the little girl who was just standing with the cookies?"

"I paid her already," he said with a stern look upon his face. Claude politely pushed open the front door to let himself in. He walked over to the kitchen table, where he slowly sat the cookies down, taking a long hard stare at Mia without saying a single word.

"What tha' fuck do you think you are doing?" she asked.

"I just wanted to see you in person," he answered.

"Well, you need to leave now," said Mia.

"Alright," he said. Claude walked to the front door as if he was about to leave, but instead, he closed the door behind him and locked it. "Oh, you thought you could just run me off like that, huh," stated Claude with a sinister laugh.

"What are you talking about, Claude?" asked Mia.

"Don't play dumb with me Mia, you know exactly what I'm talking about," he told her. Claude pointed his finger directly between her eyes. "I asked you nicely to handle the situation. But nah, you chose to curse me out and ignore all of my phone calls," said Claude. "What's the matter, Mia," he said sarcastically. "I see you ain't actin' so cocky now that we are alone."

"This is the last time I'm gonna' tell you to leave or else I'm calling the cops," stated Mia. "And they will get your ass to leave." She began feeling a little tense as she spoke with uncertainty in her voice.

"Give me that motha' fucking phone!" demanded Claude grabbing Mia's cell phone before she could dial 911. He then overpowered her and took full control. "You ain't calling no damn body," he told her. "I'm about tired of your ass anyway," said Claude.

"Nigga, let my fuckin' arm go," said Mia managing to get away from Claude's tight hold. "I was planning on having an abortion tomorrow. Just get tha' fuck out of here," she said, pointing toward the door. Mia began yelling as loud as she could as she tried moving closer to the front door to open it.

"It's too late for that," stated Claude. He looked as if the devil himself had taken over his body. Claude manhandled her with an even tighter hold, grabbing both of her arms to keep her from trying to open the front door.

"P-L-E-A-S-E! Let go me!" begged Mia. "Are you fuckin' crazy!?" she screamed.

"Funny, you weren't so scared when you were in the shopping center talking all that shit," said Claude. "I almost forgot you threaten to go to my wife with this shit, too. Apparently, you don't know who the fuck I am," he told Mia. "I tried to be reasonable with your stupid ass, but now I have to do it my way."

"H-E-L-P!" Mia screamed.

"BITCH! Shut the fuck up!" Claude's hand went across Mia's face with a loud slap.

"Claude, please don't hurt me," Mia cried nervously. She was shaking fearfully while holding one side of her face with her hand. "I'll do whatever you want," she said. "Please don't hurt me," she continued as the tears rolled down her pretty face. Mia was ready to rectify the situation any way she could to satisfy Claude's emotions.

"C'mon," she pleaded with him like a dope fiend. "I'll give you a real good blowjob. Then we could take care of the abortion together and go on with our separate lives," said Mia.

"Your ass would say anything to get me out of here," noted Claude. "You gonna' learn that playing those schoolgirl games don't get you anywhere." Claude was committed to following through with his plan. He slapped her around and then began to think about his actions, along with the consequences, from putting his hands on Mia. Claude left Mia in tears. She laid in the middle of her living room floor crying hysterically from the screaming match that just erupted.

After the hard push to the wall from Claude, Mia was now feeling pain on the left side of her body. The loud noise through the thin walls caused her next-door neighbor to call the police to Mia's apartment. The door was still unlocked and cracked open, which allowed the policemen easy access to find Mia lying on the floor of her small living room. Mia slowly began to stand to her feet as she noticed a very red bruise on her left arm, but nothing could have prepared her for the questions she was bombarded with. One officer showed much empathy for Mia by providing his business card for her to call him when she felt well enough to put in a police report of the incident. Mia was very happy to see her sister by her side. Even though Mikayla and her weren't on the best of terms, she knew that nothing could come between their sisterhood in difficult times like this one.

CHAPTER 40

A Simple "Thank You" Goes a Long Way

"Thank you, sis, for picking me up," said Mia.

"Girl, you don't have to worry," replied Mikayla. "No matter what happens between us, I will always have your back," said Mikayla. "That motha' fucka' is gonna' pay for what he did to you," she said. "No, Mikayla. Please don't try to retaliate on the count of me and get your ass in trouble," said Mia.

Mia thought of different ways she could make Claude pay for what he did to her, but it was only a matter of time before karma was going to ruin him. "Just hold on," Mia told her little sister. "He will definitely pay for what he did to me," she said with a mischievous look on her face.

"Look at you, Mia. He could have broken your arm. Your ass is lucky to be alive," Mikayla said, inspecting Mia's face once again for any injuries.

"I'm so sorry for being insensitive about your sexuality," Mia told her sister.

"Well, thank you," replied Mikayla giving her sister a big hug. Mikayla thought Claude looked a little crazy, but she didn't know he would go to the length of putting his hands on her sister. "I guess it's fair to address the elephant in the room," said Mikayla.

"What elephant?" replied Mia. She looked around the large guest room of Mikayla's apartment, trying to dodge the question.

"You need to come straight with me," Mikayla told her.

"Alright," said Mia. "Please promise me that you won't tell anybody, including mama," she begged her sister. Mia made her sister cross her heart and swear on the Holy Bible sitting on the nightstand that she wouldn't tell a soul. Mikayla obliged to her wish as she listened to the whole story of what happened to cause Mia's altercation with Claude.

"I guess he thought pushing you around could make you lose the baby," said Mikayla.

"Yup, and he will never know that his plan failed. I just hope my baby doesn't have any birth defects from the trauma of all of this," said Mia. "I understand how much you care about your unborn child, but do you really think it was wise of you to be getting pregnant while mama is breaking her back to take care of your kids?" asked Mikayla.

"It was a mistake. I wasn't trying to make any more babies," said Mia. Mikayla listed a number of ways that her sister could have protected herself from getting pregnant for the third time.

"You don't understand, Mikayla...I..." responded Mia. Before she could explain herself any further, she was interrupted.

"Just get some rest," said Mikayla speaking like a big sister. She didn't want to upset her sister and risk the conversation turning into an argument.

Nothing Beats Betrayal

"Hi THERE, LADIES," said the hostess. "Welcome to *Tony's Lasagna House*. How many will be seated?" the hostess asked.

"Just two," Jazzman told the hostess.

"Nice," said Jazzman's best friend, Tiffany. "How's the food?" she asked.

"You are going to love it," Jazzman told her. "My mama and I have been here a few times before," said Jazzman informing her friend of some of the good Italian dishes. Both Jazzman and Tiffany were seated in a booth by the window where they could see the bar from where they were sitting.

"I'm starving," said Tiffany. Jazzman was enjoying her time spent hanging out with her longtime friend. After placing their order for food and drinks, the conversation began to take an unexpected turn. "So, how has therapy been going with you and your mom?" Tiffany asked Jazzman.

"It's going good," answered Jazzman. "Things are definitely looking up for us," she said. "I think she's ready to really make a change for the better," Jazzman told her friend.

"Sounds like y'all are gonna' be best buddies pretty soon," stated Tiffany.

"She's coming around slowly in seeing the error of her ways," replied Jazzman.

"I'm really proud of you two for putting in an effort to make your relationship work," said Tiffany with a big smile. "I couldn't imagine my mama and me not talking even for a day," she added.

"Well, I'm sorry if everybody doesn't have that Mary Poppin's relationship like you and your mama have," Jazzman said. "Girl, you know I didn't mean it like that. Don't be so defensive," Tiffany told Jazzman.

"I apologize," said Jazzman. "Whenever the mother and daughter subject comes up, it just strikes a chord in me," she noted. "I guess there is a little jealousy on my part, too. But, I'm getting past it slowly now that my mother-daughter relationship is improving."

"A mother and daughter's relationship is never perfect. You should embrace the good things you do share with your mother and pass it down to your own children one day," Tiffany pointed out.

"Look at you trying to give some advice," Jazzman said with a chuckle. "Now, what handbook did you get that out of?" she playfully told her friend. "She can stop paying for those therapy sessions," said Jazzman.

"Don't be silly," laughed Tiffany. "Speaking of your mama, that lady sitting over there at the bar favors her a lot," said Tiffany.

"Girl, that's my mama!" said Jazzman. She couldn't believe her mother was sitting with the man she absolutely despised. Colleen's actions were deplorable, and Jazzman couldn't wait to confront her about it.

Jazzman had now grown horns at the top of her head that led straight to her mother's face to confront her. And Tiffany was a spectator like the others at the restaurant as she watched her best friend storm over to the bar. "That man...that man!" Jazzman repeated, unable to get out her words.

She moved her head from side-to-side in frustration as she rewinded her childhood memories in her head of her mother's ex-boyfriend, Henry, sexually abusing her. "I can't believe you are sitting here having a drink with this piece of shit," said Jazzman. "I thought we were in a better place," cried Jazzman.

"Jazz, honey, let's go outside. It's not what you think," said Colleen. Jazzman ignored her mother's gestures while the man she hated sat there in silence with a smirk painted on his face.

"I don't want to talk to you," stated Jazzman. "How stupid was I to believe that you could change," she said. "You ain't nothing but an alcoholic, drug-addicted bitch!" shouted Jazzman.

Meanwhile, the entire crowd focused their attention on the mother and daughter as if they were watching a drama movie. "After all this man has done to us, you have the nerve to sit here having a good ole time talking and drinking with him. Not to mention, disrespecting your marriage for this fucking pervert," Jazzman told her mother.

"Jazzman," said Colleen. "Stop making a scene," her mother demanded. Colleen wondered where in the hell was security when she needed them. "If you would just let me get a word in," said Colleen.

"I have nothing to say to you or him," she said, pointing to the man she had hated for years. "What happened to the drug addiction meetings?" Jazzman questioned her. "You are probably back using again, too," she assumed.

"That's enough of embarrassing yourself," stated Colleen. "If you can't talk to me alone, you need to leave," she told her daughter.

"I'm done here," replied Jazzman. "Everyone carry on, because this show is over," she said. "I'm going to leave this liar and child pedophile in peace," stated Jazzman as she pointed to both her mother and Henry. He then stood up as if he was going to hit Jazzman, but Colleen stepped in to hold him back.

"C'mon on, Tiffany. Let's get out of here," she said.

The Lies You Tell...

DESPITE KNOWING THAT Claude was still out there somewhere; Mia was back at home. She thought to herself, he was probably waiting in the bushes to get her. Although Mikayla had taken care of her like she was a helpless child, she needed to get back home to her privacy. She had a lot of secrets to continue to hide.

At home, she could think clearer and come up with a resolution to her problems. Then, suddenly, a knock at the door, *Knock...Knock.*

Mia was horrified when she heard the knock at the door. She began turning off all of the lights and the television to act like no one was home. She was afraid that it could be Claude at the door coming back to cause more harm. But, Mia suddenly realized she couldn't go through life being scared of the unknown. She checked the peephole, and there stood Brad at her doorstep looking as good as he'd ever looked.

Her first initial reaction was to be mad, but she was glad to see him at the same time. Mia had missed her man, so she opened the door knowing she would have to explain her broken arm.

"Hey," said Brad. "I was in the neighborhood and decided to stop by," he told her.

"Sure you were," replied Mia.

"What happened?" asked Brad. He saw that Mia's arm was wrapped in a splint.

"Oh, yeah," said Mia. "I was in a car accident," she told him.

"I can see why you've been avoiding my calls. You weren't up for talking…huhn," said Brad.

"Yeah, I just needed some time to myself," replied Mia.

"I didn't see any dents on your car. You would think with a sprung arm, your car would have been totaled out," implied Brad.

"Actually, I was riding in the car with my sister, and believe me, her car had taken a beaten," she said. "But, thank God we are okay, and her car can be replaced," stated Mia. Her fables were becoming normal to the extent that she was starting to believe her own lies.

"Well, I'm glad that you are okay. Because I didn't know why you would disappear just like that," said Brad. He then started looking around the small apartment. He had never seen the inside of it until now. Brad acted like inspector Gadget, looking around the nicely decorated apartment. He then came across a picture of Mia with two cute little caramel, complexion kids that looked just like her sitting on the fireplace's mantle. He picked up the picture to take a closer look at the loving-looking family. "Hmm…I take it these are your kids?" he asked.

"Well, you didn't ask me if I had any," replied Mia. "But yes, those are my babies, Jacob and Santana," Mia answered with a smile. "They have been staying with my mama in Lake Charles, Louisiana. She wanted them out there to keep her company,"

Mia continued to cover her tracks. It was the perfect time for Mia to see if Brad even liked the idea of having any kids of his own since the conversation had never come up before. "How do you feel about me having kids?" she asked him.

"I have no problems with you having kids," said Brad. "I have two nieces that are adorable," he told Mia.

"Do you want any kids of your own one day?" Mia asked curiously.

"Yeah, in the future," he answered. Mia felt that Brad was answering all of her questions with a passing score, but she still found it difficult to tell him that she was having his unborn child.

"What's with all the baby questions?" asked Brad. "Are you pregnant?" he bluntly asked.

"Do I look pregnant?" she asked.

"Well, you are starting to look like you picked up some weight since the last time I saw you," he answered.

"Yes, I'm pregnant," Mia blurted out. "With your baby," she told him.

"You are pregnant with my baby!?" he repeated and asked. "Wow," he said.

Brad was thinking about how it could have happened when he had used protection most of the times they've had sex. "You just gonna' leave me now that I'm pregnant," Mia said, noticing Brad's facial expression.

"Nah, I'm not going to leave you, baby," stated Brad. "I'm just thinking," he told her.

"Thinking about what?" asked Mia.

"When could I have gotten you pregnant?" asked Brad. "You weren't on the pill?!" he questioned Mia.

"Now you want to question me about being on the pill. You weren't questioning me about shit when you had your dick all up in my pussy," stated Mia. Brad remembered that he was just as irresponsible as Mia for using the pullout method instead of wearing a condom one hundred percent of the time.

"How many months are you," he questioned Mia. Of course, Mia had the months already calculated in her head to cover the lies she told.

"I'm ten and a half weeks pregnant," she said. When in fact, she was much further along.

"Come here," said Brad. "Girl, I'm going to take good care of you and this baby," he told Mia as he rubbed her barely showing pregnant belly. "You don't have to worry about anything," he said, sounding totally opposite from Claude's response to Mia's news.

"What did the doctor say about the baby being in the car accident?" he asked. Brad was now very concerned for what he thought was his unborn fetus.

"Well, my doctor said that I should be fine," replied Mia. She had Brad thinking of a whole new life after hearing she was carrying his baby.

"You are coming home with me," stated Brad. "I'm going to keep you safe at least until this baby is born because I don't need any more mishaps with you," he said, speaking from a caring man's position. "My chef will start you off with a healthy dinner tonight, and we could watch a good movie at the house in the theater room. Just grab a few things and let's get outta' here," demanded Brad.

Mia was in awe of Brad's take-charge attitude, wondering why she was so paranoid in the first place about telling him when it seemed like a cakewalk.

Tough Love

"HEY SIS, HOW are you doing?" Colleen sounded apologetic through the phone. "Colleen," answered Tina. "I'm not in the mood for your shit today," Tina warned her sister.

"I understand, sis," said Colleen. "You don't have to worry about me getting out of line with you," she stated. "Sis," Colleen called her sister. "I do apologize for not taking your advice sooner about Malcolm," she told Tina. "That motha' fucka' is still on drugs," she said.

"What happened?" asked Tina. Colleen gave her sister, Tina, all the details of Malcolm and her conversation, including the part about how she got the money to pay their past due mortgage payments.

"I couldn't believe my eyes," Colleen told her. "The man I married would never walk out of the house without his cologne on, and his clothes ironed," she said. "That's how I knew something was wrong."

"Well, you know what they say about them drugs," replied Tina. "It takes over your mind, body, and soul completely. It will make you do things that you would have never thought of in your wildest dreams," Tina told her sister.

The more Tina talked; she could hear Colleen trying to hold back her tears. Colleen felt that her life was crashing down on her before she'd even gotten a moment to really enjoy her marriage. Also, Tina wasn't showing much sympathy at all for her emotional breakdown. "Well, you did the right thing by putting his ass out," Tina commended her sister for having the courage to do what she did. "And that brother of his must be a saint for loaning you that much money," stated Tina.

"You know I had to beg his ass for the money," said Colleen. "He was fed up with Malcolm's ass so much that he didn't want anything else to do with him.

"And who can blame him," added Tina. "Well, he only loaned me the money because I told him that I didn't know anybody else who would let me borrow such a large sum of money. He also thought that I was a good woman for his brother when we talked at the wedding," said Colleen. "Boy, was I grateful for the three-thousand dollars. Do you know how much interest I would have to pay on a loan like that?"

"I'm quite sure it would be a lot," replied Tina. "Well, at least he's got family with some money," she said.

"Yeah, his brother is loaded with that high-power attorney-type money. He thought it was messed up the way Malcolm did me by not paying the mortgage," noted Colleen. "And I sure wasn't going to ask you for the money knowing your financial woos. Tina praised her sister for thinking of her in the process as she worked on other ways to get the money.

"You definitely don't need somebody like him bringing you back down," stated Tina. Colleen thought about what her sister was saying, but telling her own secret of drinking while her marriage had been in a slump wasn't one she was going to reveal to all.

"I feel like a failure," said Colleen.

"You aren't a failure," replied Tina. "Your trials and tribulations in life are what make you stronger. Sure, Malcolm was in your life for only a short time, but you learned a lot in those few minutes," said Tina trying to light up the mood.

"You are right about that," Colleen agreed with her sister Tina.

"Please take it slow the next time around," advised Tina. Tina hoped her sister was taking notes for the next beau she meets. Colleen knew that her older sister was so good at helping everyone else with their problems she lacked opening up to others about her own personal issues.

"How's everything with you and the family?" asked Colleen.

"We are fine," said Tina.

"Are you sure about that?" asked Colleen. "Yes," said Tina failing to mention her migraine headaches that were becoming annoying.

"Besides the constant problem of trying to bring Mia up to par with being a responsible adult," stated Tina.

"Mia is still up to her same old mess," replied Colleen. "As always, avoiding my calls, not giving me money for her kids, all those things are making me sick," said Colleen.

"Maybe you need to show her better than you can tell her," stated Colleen. "Give those kids back to her, and she will wake up then," Colleen told her sister.

"You sound like James now," replied Tina.

"Well, listen to your husband and show Mia some tough love," said Colleen.

"She wouldn't know what to do if she saw us standing at her doorstep with the kids bags packed and everything," said Tina.

"That's exactly what you should do," Colleen said encouraging her sister. Meanwhile, she thought about how she would interact with her own daughter after what had gone down at the restaurant. Colleen felt ashamed of herself for giving Jazzman the impression that she'd turned back into the old person she used to be. But, she wasn't going to unload anymore of her problems onto her sister for open criticism at the time. Colleen thought it was time to quit holding back and try to make it right once again with her daughter, Jazzman.

Ain't Nothing to It, But to Do It

MIA HAD THE world at her feet. Or so it seemed, as she lived her luxurious lifestyle. Brad showered her with everything she needed from a full day spa treatment to a housekeeping crew. He waited on her hand and feet including a chef at her beck and call. Mia had more than a pregnant woman could ever ask for. Even though Brad traveled out of state a few days a week for his part-time job as a sports commentator, he made frequent calls home in order to make sure his woman was taking her prenatal pills and eating healthy.

She thought his kindness was very nurturing as she realized she'd never had a man to treat her with so much respect as Brad did. It was refreshing, but then again, Mia felt guilty day-by-day as she rehearsed the plot in her head to trap the man she was beginning to fall deeply in love with. Mia was starting to think that Brad was just too nice of a man to shatter his world if he ever found out later down the road that this unborn child wasn't actually his own flesh and blood.

Mia may have done some horrible things throughout her life, but she'd never done such a vicious thing as this before. Although Mia had been fatigued lately, she wanted to at least keep some dignity by working a little longer before she'd put in her final two-week notice. Plus, she was getting lonely in the big ass house, which gave her too much idle time to think about all of her transgressions.

***

"*Concord Cable Co.* This is Mia. How can I help you today?"

"Listen here, this is the second time y'all charge me for some bullshit porn movies I didn't order. I am a Christian woman," said the customer.

"Okay, ma'am, what is your account number?" Mia asked the woman.

"It's 1---6981. Ella Faye Jackson is the name on the account," she sighed.

"This bitch knows she ordered these movies or at least someone did," Mia spoke with the phone on mute. She then pressed the unmute button to speak back to the customer in a calm tone. "Well, after reviewing your account, I see that *Urban Fat Pussy Cats* was ordered two hours apart from *Three Men and a Penis*, Mia told her, stating the time and date.

"There's no way in hell I ordered those damn movies. Plus, I'm at work during that time of the day," said the woman.

"Are you sure someone else didn't order them?" Mia asked her.

"It's just my husband and me," replied the woman. "Jeffrey, Jeffrey," the woman yelled out. She loudly questioned him regarding the time frame of when the movies were ordered.

"Huhn," the man replied back.

"Don't huhn me," the woman repeated her question.

"I don't remember," the man responded. The customer and her husband spoke loudly as they carried on with their conversation as if Mia wasn't holding the phone on the other end of the line.

"Wait a minute, I was at home on that day," the man told his wife.

"I'mma' beat yo' ass, Jeffrey," said the woman. Meanwhile, Mia was in the background cracking up laughing. "Let me call y'all back," stated the woman abruptly hanging up the phone in Mia's ear.

"Damn, these customers are crazy as hell," said Mia. She then continued doodling in her drawing book as she waited for the next call before being called into the human resource department office. Mia figured the manager wanted to speak to her regarding the extra time she'd taken off for medical leave.

"Hi, Ms. Mary," Mia spoke politely to the manager of the HR department.

"Mia, I called you in my office to inform you of some cutbacks that the company will have to take at this time," she told Mia. For some strange reason, Mia's stomach was beginning to turn as she continued listening to the manager speak.

"Unfortunately, the rumors around the office were true if you heard them," the manager told her. "We are going to have to downsize certain departments immediately due to these budget cuts, which means that customer service is one of our departments that must be downsized as of now," she explained. "We are letting you go today," the manager stated without any hesitation. Although the manager was straightforward, Mia felt really good to hear her say how much she was appreciated for the hard work she'd put in for the company. But, Mia was also in disbelief of how many others would now be out of work that really needed their job. "Are we supposed to get some sort of severance package for being laid off?" Mia asked the manager. Mia wanted to secure herself so she wouldn't leave empty-handed.

"Well, some employees will receive a severance package depending on the number of years they've been with the company," she told Mia. "But, in your case Mia," she said, looking down at Mia's paperwork. "Unfortunately, you haven't worked with the company long enough to receive a severance package. But, you shouldn't have any problems receiving your unemployment benefits while you seek other employment," the manager said to Mia. "And please continue to keep us updated. You never know when the company may start rehiring again," she informed Mia.

Mia thanked the manager for giving her the opportunity to work for the company, but she also felt a little bitter-sweet feeling as she packed her stuff and headed out the glass doors.

***

On the drive home, all Mia could think about were her kids, Jacob and Santana, and all the time she really wanted to spend with them, but work would always get in the way of their quality time together. Now that Mia was jobless with money, she could spend more time with her kids like she'd always wanted to do. But, Mia was very afraid of the consequences she would suffer if she'd ever lost her man and was left alone with three children to fend for if her plot was to blow up in her face. Mia thought about telling Brad the truth, but it would now be a closed discussion due to the fact that she had just become unemployed. She felt that it would ruin any hope of him staying with her once he'd found out the truth. Mia was finally thinking like an adult, but she wondered if it was too late to get her life back on track.

"I got it!" Mia spoke out loud to herself. Mia knew her man would be crushed if she was to unexpectedly have a miscarriage, but she figured he would deal with the loss better than finding out his child wasn't his in the first place. "If I suddenly had a miscarriage, it would be devastating, but it would also bring us even closer," she said, thinking aloud. Mia figured if she went the empathy route that her plan would work much better. "I'm sure he would suggest that my kids move in with us after suffering such terrible loss," assumed Mia.

All that was left to do was for Mia to put her plan in motion as soon as possible. Mia thought that Brad's weekly travel wouldn't be a problem at all to schedule the procedure around the days he's gone. Mia hated herself for adding Brad into all of her crazy drama, but she had to resolve this dilemma the best way she knew how to save herself from further damage. Before Mia could get home, she was on her cellular phone calling a local clinic to get all the information she needed.

It Was All a Big Misunderstanding

COLLEEN WAS HOPING Jazzman would find it in her heart to forgive her once again. She called her daughter several times a day, leaving numerous messages on her voicemail, but Jazzman refused to answer any of her calls regardless of how much she'd begged. Colleen finally had enough with Jazzman avoiding her calls. She even had her niece, Mikayla, to call her on three-way, and when that didn't work, there was only one option left to do.

Colleen was now standing on the front porch of Jazzman's best friend's house at the crack of dawn, banging on the door like a crazy mad woman.

"Ms. Colleen," said Tiffany whipping the cold out of her eyes. "Do you know what time it is?"

"Yes, I do," replied Colleen.

"Well, you should know you can't come here trying to knock down people's door at this time of the morning. My mother is trying to get some sleep before she has to wake up for work in a few hours," said Tiffany.

"I need to speak to Jazzman," said Colleen.

"Jazzman isn't here," replied Tiffany.

"Please don't play with me this morning," stated Colleen. "Her car is parked right there in the driveway," she told Tiffany.

"Well, she's..." said Tiffany being immediately interrupted.

"Well, she's what…" repeated Colleen. "She what…didn't come home last night from a date," Colleen helped Tiffany out with her next lie. "Please just let me speak to my daughter," Colleen pleaded on Tiffany's front porch. She hoped maybe Tiffany could hear her cries through her voice.

"Hold on, Ms. Colleen. Let me see if she wants to talk to you," said Tiffany.

"Thank you so much for helping me out," Colleen told her.

"Well, I can't make her talk to you if she doesn't want to," Tiffany advised Colleen. But, Colleen was thankful for Tiffany even trying to get her friend to communicate with her after knowing how badly she'd hurt her so many times. After an hour and a half wait, Jazzman finally met her mother on the front porch, and she wasn't happy at all with her mother's boldness to show up at someone else's home causing havoc. Colleen felt she had to get things straight because the look on her daughter's face showed a sign that there wouldn't be a next time for her mother's unpredictable behavior. They both sat in the lawn chairs on the porch to talk.

"Mama, are you on drugs again?" Jazzman asked. It was the first question that popped into her head? "Please be honest with me," she said.

"Hell, N-O!" answered Colleen.

"Well, you were there with that drug dealer, Henry. Have you forgotten what he did to me," said Jazzman.

"No, I haven't," said Colleen.

"Then why were you hanging out with him?" asked Jazzman.

"Damn, where do I start," stated Colleen.

"How about the part from when I saw you at the restaurant with Henry," replied Jazzman.

"But, it's more to the story," stated Colleen as she fidgeted with her fingers.

"Hmm," said Jazzman with a confused facial expression. Colleen was trying to gather her thoughts together before she explained everything to her daughter.

"Jazzman," she said. "I'm absolutely clean and haven't used any kind of hard drugs since my last stint in rehab. And that's the honest to God knows truth," she told her daughter. "But, on the other hand, Malcolm has relapsed recently," stated Colleen. "He sold a lot of my expensive stuff for drugs, including my wedding ring. I almost lost my house in foreclosure because he wasn't paying any of the mortgage payments," said Colleen.

"Well, that's what you get for marrying that man from your drug and alcohol meetings," stated Jazzman. "With all due respect, I am very sorry for what has happened in your marriage, mama...I was starting to like you and Malcolm as a couple."

"I have learned so much even at my age now," noted Colleen. "I can't believe how I was so naïve."

"Maybe, you just wanted a man so bad that you didn't even realize what you were getting yourself into," Jazzman told her. She was still trying to understand the reasoning behind her mother being seen with Henry. So far, the pieces of the puzzle still weren't fitting from what she was hearing.

"When I saw you with Henry, were you still with Malcolm?" Jazzman asked curiously. "No, he had moved out by then. And I was very upset with the world," said Colleen.

"And getting back with Henry was the right thing to do mama?" she asked, confused and seeking a healing answer.

"First of all, I didn't get back with Henry," Colleen stated. "I just wanted some closure with everything in my life," she explained. "I didn't even talk to him after he threw me out of his house years ago. But, now I see it was a mistake because it cost me my relationship with you," stated Colleen. "Plus, Henry didn't have any remorse for what he did to us," Colleen told her daughter.

"Mama, you should have known that you can't talk sense into crazy," said Jazzman. "So why were you drinking with him?" she questioned her mother.

"I was drinking a sparkling water," noted Colleen. "You should have said something when I came over," said Jazzman.

"You didn't let me get in a word edge-wise. I'm sure you remember that you went crazy after seeing me sitting with Henry. You weren't trying to hear me out at all," stated Colleen.

"No, I wasn't," Jazzman said, thinking about that day. "I was just too mad, and I definitely wanted you and him to know it," she said. "But, my gut feeling was telling me that it had to be a reason why you were out with that horrible man. I am so happy now that my gut feeling was right," said Jazzman.

"It was all a big misunderstanding," added Colleen. "Henry makes me sick to my stomach, but I also know what he's capable of doing. The man is ruthless. I didn't want him coming after me or you if we would have teamed up on him. I was only protecting you from him," stated Colleen.

"Mama, thanks for explaining," said Jazzman. "I feel so much better now that we have talked," she said.

"I feel the same way, too," Colleen responded. "Now, what am I going to do in that big house all by myself," she said, smiling at her daughter. "Would you like to move back home with your mama?"

"Sure, I will," Jazzman replied back. "It's expensive to live out on your own," she said. Jazzman thought about how she has to pay rent to Tiffany's mother. "Plus, I can really save some money moving back in with you," stated Jazzman. This time around, Colleen was going to cherish every single moment she had with daughter instead of knocking her down with her negative attitude every chance she would get.

Can't Take Tha Hood Out Tha' Girl

MIA PULLED OFF *her plan without a hitch.*

She waited patiently on Brad to take his flight to NYC for his three-day workweek. Mia knew Brad's routine like the back of her hand, so she waited until he was settled into his hotel suite before later calling to inform him of the bad news. The so-called spotting she'd been experiencing had gotten worse, causing her to have to drive herself to the emergency room.

There Mia found out by the ER doctor that she had indeed suffered a miscarriage. She cried over the phone as she spoke to her man. As soon as Brad was told the news, he immediately wanted to rush home, but his flight was delayed due to weather conditions. "Are you okay?" "Do you need anything?" Brad asked a series of questions feeling like he was in a helpless state due to the distance between his woman and him." Mia managed to calm herself down to answer her man's questions.

"Yes, I have the medicine the doctor prescribed. If I need anything, I promise I will ask Nina," stated Mia.

"Nina's the best maid in town, and she will make sure you are taken care of until I get home," added Brad. "Just hold on, baby. I will be home as soon as possible," he said with an assurance in his voice. Once Brad got home, he felt very sad for the loss of his unborn child, especially after preparing himself for a major role into fatherhood.

Although he continued to console his woman, Brad prayed that Mia could eventually move on from this horrific experience. He continued to give her flowers and sweet hallmark cards to uplift her spirit through those sad days. Mia had been playing the role like an academy award winning actress until she decided it was time to slowly lay off the tears after enough time had passed. Meanwhile, Brad thought it would make his woman very happy once she saw her brand-new white Range Rover parked outside with a big red bow across the top of the hood.

Mia wanted to release the truth at that moment, but she'd never been treated like a princess in her entire life, and she wasn't going to let her fairy tale life come to an end in a blink of an eye. Mia had taken the keys from her man like a sixteen-year-old teenager who'd just received her first vehicle. She then excitedly checked out the exterior and interior as if she was on a scavenger hunt.

***

On a nice sunny day, Mia had ridden through her old neighborhood in her new truck hoping to see some of her old friends hanging out around the hood. She had stopped at the local convenience store where she felt like a rich bitch getting out of her truck to walk into the store while everyone stared at her up and down. Mia felt a little conceded, twisting from side to side as she walked back to her truck.

"Mia, girl, is that you," a squeaky male voice called out from far away. Mia turned her head around to see it was in fact her old friend from the hood that she had known since childhood.

"G-dog!" said Mia. "Boy, what's been up?" she asked him.

"Nothing much," he answered. "Same ole shit' always up to no good," stated G-dog.

"Boy, you better slow your ass down then," said Mia.

"Yeah, I ain't trying to end up like ya' boy on tha' run," noted G-dog.

"My boy," repeated Mia with a smirk on her face.

"Yo' boy Derrick," he told her.

"Derrick ain't my man," replied Mia.

"C'mon Mia, don't act like you don't remember how you and Derrick used to get down," he said. "Is that you?" G-dog asked. He had ventured off the topic, pointing to the shiny white SUV truck Mia had just pumped gas in.

"Of course, it's me, who else would it be," stated Mia.

"Damn, I didn't know you were rolling like that now. You must have picked it up straight off the showroom floor," stated G-dog.

"Yeah, I got it like that," replied Mia. She was still on a high from her boyfriend, Brad, surprising her with it as a gift. "Hmm…Is Derrick is on the run?" asked an inquisitive Mia.

"Yeah, that nigga' got caught with ten kilos of dope. He was out on bond when he skipped town," said G-dog. Mia had thought about her most recent encounter with him that left her mad as hell at him for leaving her only fifty dollars the next morning after she had just given him the best sex he may have ever had in his life.

"I just recently seen Derrick," noted Mia. She purposely left out their night of passion. "He was telling me how he was about to do it big in tha' dope game. Nino Brown-style," added Mia.

"Nino Brown, my ass. That nigga' is a fugitive now," noted G-dog. "And when they catch his ass, he ain't gon' ever see the free world. With the case, he caught for assaulting that dike bitch over at *Scores* strip club in a feud over her damn stripper girlfriend and this here dope case is enough shit to get that nigga' locked up for a long time," stated G-dog. Hearing about

Derrick's run in's with the law wasn't new, but this time it was different because one of his involvements may have included Mia's sister.

Mia was very surprised to learn that her sister, Mikayla, could have possibly been in an altercation with Derrick over Roxy's whore ass, she thought. Even though Mia wanted to call out her old friend for disrespecting the victim with his derogatory name-calling, she couldn't be too mad at him or her sister for keeping it all a secret. For one, G-dog didn't know that the dike bitch he was talking about was Mia's sister, and Mikayla probably hadn't told everyone about her sexuality at the time when the incident occurred.

Mia figured there could only be one reason why her sister wouldn't ever mention something so serious like this to her. "That explains it all," Mia thought out loud. She was thinking the black eye that her sister, Mikayla, was sporting at the time of her Aunt Colleen's wedding could have possibly come from Derrick.

"Huh," said G-dog.

"That explains why Derrick always used to say that nobody could hold him, not even the Po-Po's," responded Mia. She didn't think that it was necessary to let G-Dog know that the dike bitch he was referring to was probably her sister, plus she was a little embarrassed to let anyone know that her sister was a homosexual. In a way, she felt like it was her fault that she and her sister led such a separate life growing up.

Mia and Mikayla were total opposites with different social groups that sometimes caused a wedge in their sister bond. Mia was the popular hood girl with more guys after her than she could keep track of. On the other hand, Mikayla was a quiet nerd with only a few friends who sat around reading books. Mia thought if she had taken out more time with her sister over the years, somehow things would have turned out different with her encounter with Derrick. "Damn, that's messed up," stated Mia. "Derrick has never struck me as the woman-beater type."

"But, from what I heard, it was that bitch who took a swing at him first, and he knocked her ass out," stated G-dog. "You wanna' look and act like a man, then you should take it like a man when you get knocked the fuck out, which was G-dog's motto." Mia halfway agreed with G-dog's one-sided story.

"I see you are still out here hustling," said Mia.

"You know it... still nickel and diming it for now. But, I got my own plans lined up, too," he told her.

"Boy, you are gonna' land your ass in jail," stated Mia.

"Nah, I think more strategic than that dumb ass nigga, Derrick. He kept hanging out at *Club Hennessey*, knowing damn well that old ass man, Henry, was observing his ass the whole time. He was balling out of control, buying every damn body drinks and shit." And just when Derrick's ass was starting to dip into some of his territory, the old man Henry tipped off the police and set his ass up," noted G-dog. "What nigga, do you know hangs out at the club where his competition owns it?".

"Yeah, that sounds crazy," added Mia.

"I warned his ass not to get too close to that nigga, Henry. But, he thought just because that nigga taught him everything he knew about the game, he could trust the mother fucka' just like the rest of them stupid ass fools who went to jail behind Henry's scandalous ass," said G-dog.

"That name sounds familiar," noted Mia. "I think my aunt and him used to live together back in the days," stated Mia. She vaguely described his tall, dark, unattractive features. "If we are talking about the same dude, he is definitely a damn snake in the grass," she said.

"Yeah, that's him," said G-dog agreeing with Mia.

"He does some real estate shit too," said Mia.

"Yeah, that's one nigga' that was into any and everything that would make his ass a dollar," stated G-dog. "But, I guess somebody got fed up with his dirty ass and slit that nigga's neck wide open just the other day. They left his ass dead in the back office of his night club still with the blindfold on,"

"They did what!" said Mia. She listened to G-dog give her some juicy gossip in front of the convenience store. She couldn't wait to inform her Aunt Colleen about the death of her old monstrous boyfriend.

"This dope game is real out here," stated G-dog. "Now I'm next in line to get mine since all these fools are dead or in jail," he said.

"And, you are planning a takeover?" asked Mia.

"Hell yeah," replied G-dog. "First of all, you can't let everybody in yo' business like Derrick'em used to do. And second, you can't trust no damn body in this business," G-dog gave Mia the four one-one on how to stay in the game. "Third, make as much loot as you can in a short period of time, then invest your shit with some legit profitable businesses. I gotta' do something, because I'm tired of fucking with this weed," G-dog told Mia. "By the way, did you wanna' get some from me?" he asked.

"Nah, I'm good," replied Mia.

"I bet you are good," said G-dog. "Smoking on some of that good shit from outta' Cali," he told her. "I would be too if I could afford to ride around in a hundred-thousand dollar SUV truck like that," G-dog said with a chuckle.

"Just be careful out here in these streets," said Mia. "Shi-t-e-d, all the time, baby," stated G-dog using his dirty south Houstonian slang as he spoke to Mia. "I'm always watching my back around these wards," he said.

G-dog looked around from left to right as if he was very paranoid. He was just like all the other d-boys in the hood that constantly had to watch their back for the police and other hoodlums.

"Here, take my number," said G-dog. He took out a pen and an old receipt from his baggy pants to write his cell phone number on it. "If you need anything, don't hesitate to give me a holler," said the short, curly head, tattooed covered, G-dog.

As Mia drove off, she could read the words from G-dog's lips: "Damn, that sundress is fitting right on her ass."

She waved goodbye.

Can We All Just Get Along

MIA THOUGHT THAT taking her sister and cousin to *Fun Zone Entertainment Plaza*, where Brad had taken her on their second date, would be lots of fun for her and the girls to enjoy themselves.

"Damn, we haven't hung out like this in a long time," said Mikayla taking a sip of her frozen daiquiri.

"Mia, I enjoyed beating your ass in air hockey," laughed Jazzman.

"Girl, I let you win," said Mia.

"Nah Mia, Jazzman beat your ass. It was fair and square. Just admit it, Mia, you ain't good in anything that requires a puck, ball, racquet, and whatever else," said Mikayla.

"I think you named them all," Jazzman said with a chuckle.

"Arrr…I see y'all are teaming up on me," said Mia. "But, Kayla," said Mia calling her sister by her nickname. You know I whopped your butt in bowling," she told her sister.

"C'mon, I wouldn't use the term whopped, but more like barely beat me," said Mikayla laughing at her sister's exaggeration.

"Jazzman's ass just might be one of those freaks of nature. I bet she can't even explain why she's good at everything," noted Mia.

"Mia, I would have beaten you in bowling like I used to if you hadn't used that grandma technique. Throwing the bowl from between your legs isn't fair," stated Mikayla.

"Don't be such a sore loser lil' sis," stated Mia.

"No, you are a cheater," complained Mikayla.

Damn, Cuz," said Jazzman. "Let Mia have her one moment of victory," laughed Jazzman.

"And Jazz, you better stop throwing your under-hand jabs before y'all both be catching a cab back home," Mia told them in a playful tone of voice.

"And you gonna' be right there with us catching the cab if you don't stop downing those mojitos like that," laughed Jazzman.

"Yeah, I need to stop, huhn," said Mia.

"Yes, you need to stop," stated Mikayla looking at her sister with the side-eye. She was wondering why Mia was drinking while she was pregnant in the first place, but she wanted to respect her sister's wishes of keeping quiet about her pregnancy until she told everyone herself. "I don't think it's healthy for you to be drinking like this," Mikayla told her as she looked downward at her sister's belly. After Mia had caught onto what Mikayla was insinuating with her comment, she knew it was time for her to tell them about the bad news as well.

"There's something that I haven't told y'all," stated Mia.

"And what might that be," added Mikayla. Mia explained the whole sad story of how she was almost four months pregnant and had a sudden miscarriage, just how she'd told it to Brad. Mikayla and Jazzman took the news hard. They felt sorry that their loved one had to go through her miscarriage alone.

"Oh Mia, I am so sorry about your miscarriage," Jazzman told her cousin. "Why didn't you call me?" asked Mikayla.

"I don't know," said Mia. "I just didn't feel like talking to anyone after it happened," said Mia. "It's a horrible feeling to lose a child that you've invested so much of your love into. I always imagined if it was going to be a boy or a girl and wondering who he or she would look like. That's one reason why I wanted us to hang out and have some fun because I was tired of sitting around the house thinking about the miscarriage," stated Mia. "Plus, Brad didn't think it was healthy for us to continue dwelling since it was only bringing us further down," she said.

"So, your new boyfriend, Brad, would have been your baby's daddy?" asked a curious Jazzman. Mikayla looked at her sister to see how she would answer that million-dollar question.

"Yes, of course," answered Mia. "Enough of the baby talk already," said Mia. "We are out to have some good ole fashion fun and got damn it lets get back to it," she told the girls. "Bartender," Mia called him over. "My sister here needs another drink," she said.

"I'll take a tequila," Mikayla told him. "You are sure in a generous mood," Mikayla told her sister. "I'm just used to picking up the tab for your broke ass," laughed Mikayla.

"Girl, Mia isn't broke now. She seems to be balling now with her rich boyfriend," stated Jazzman.

"Yeah, she did pick us up in a brand-new Range Rover, so I guess it's fair to say he ain't stingy with his money," noted Mikayla with a little jealousy in her voice.

"Damn Mia, your ass lucked up big time," said Jazzman. "I need a man with some money myself," she told Mia. "Does he sell drugs?" she asked her cousin in a low whisper.

"No, Jazzman, he is a retired professional NBA player," noted Mia.

"A Pro-Basketball player!" Jazzman said with a big smile on her face.

"He's property alone makes two of this building," stated Mia.

"Well, you two should now get married and have a cute little family with you, him, and your kids," stated Mikayla. "You do remember that you have two kids by the names of Jacob and Santana," Mikayla called out Mia.

"In due time, there will definitely be a future wedding," stated Mia. "As far as my kids are concerned, you don't have to worry about them because they will be coming to live with me very soon," Mia stated with an attitude. Jazzman could definitely tell that the two sister's conversation was becoming an argument whether than a little sarcastic humor. She didn't know if it was the alcohol talking or just the sisters bickering like they usually did. But, whatever it was, she didn't like to see her cousins fighting with each other.

"Hey, Mikayla isn't that your friend Roxy?" asked Jazzman.

"Where?" asked Mikayla looking around, trying to see if it's really her.

"Look, over there in the restaurant area," said Jazzman. Mikayla was still looking around, unable to find her girlfriend.

"Over there," Mia said, pointing in the direction of where she saw Roxy sitting. "Are you blind Kayla, looking over to your right in the booth section?" asked Mia.

"Hold up, that is Roxy hugged up in the corner with that bitch," stated Mikayla. "Man, this is the last time that girl makes me look stupid. I'm going over there to let that hoe know what's up."

"Mikayla, you need to control yourself before you walk over there. Girl, I'm not trying to go to jail tonight or get my ass kicked out of this place," stated Mia.

Jazzman wanted to give her cousin Mikayla some advice about assuming the worse and then making an ass out of yourself when you find out the truth, but Mikayla wasn't trying to hear anything at that time. She couldn't blame her cousin for the way she was feeling as she thought about herself in the same position when she thought her mother had betrayed her.

"No, this is the third time Roxy has disrespected me. I'm fed up with her shit," said Mikayla. Mia reminded her sister that she was smart enough to handle the situation in a respectful matter than making a scene for everyone to notice.

"You should pull her to the side and ask her where do you two stand in your relationship," Mia advised her sister.

"Hmm…" said Mikayla appearing to be listening to her sister talk some sense into her head.

"Please don't go over there acting like a donkey," begged Mia.

"Yeah, yeah, I hear you," Mikayla told her sister as she watched her woman intimately interact with another woman.

"Listen to your sister," said Jazzman. Although Mikayla felt like a time bomb ticking, she surprised herself by taking her big sister's advice. Now that Mikayla was face to face with her woman, and the expression on Roxy's face looked like she had seen a ghost.

"How's the food?" asked Mikayla.

"It was delicious," Roxy said sarcastically. "Are you creeping up on me?" she asked Mikayla.

"No, I had no idea that you were here until my cousin Jazzman noticed you were here," said Mikayla. "Is it possible your girl could release you so we can go somewhere to talk?" Mikayla asked in a calm matter. She noticed how Ginger held onto Roxy's hand as if they were together.

"I'm not going anywhere with you right now. Do you ever get tired of questioning my every move?" asked Roxy. "You ain't my damn mama," she told Mikayla.

Mikayla could clearly see that she wasn't going to get anywhere trying to speak to Roxy in a civilized matter.

"Well, you and this chicken head can continue holding hands, but I want you and your shit out of my house tonight," Mikayla said in an authoritative tone of voice. "And maybe, this bisexual bitch will let you move in with her," stated Mikayla.

"First of all, who are you calling a chicken head, bitch?" said Ginger. "And you are a fat ass wanna' be Halley Berry, bitch," Ginger butted in, referring to Mikayla's tampered-styled haircut.

"You can't make me move because I pay the bills there too, you know," stated Roxy. "Both of our names are on the lease, and I'll be damned if you try putting me out," said Roxy.

"Fuck you, Roxy. You cheat on me, and all you have to say is that you aren't moving out. What about, 'I'm sorry' or 'let's talk about it,'" said Mikayla. "You ain't nothing but a scandalous, selfish bitch," she told Roxy.

"We ain't gonna' be too many of yo' bitches," stated Ginger.

"Y'all are some crazy hoes," said Mikayla. "It's funny how a bitch who gets butt-ass naked for a living can get mad when somebody calls her a 'bitch'. Y'all are both some stanky hoes."

"Excuse me ladies, but could you please keep it down with the loud talking and the swearing around the customers," said the manager. "We don't want to have to ask you to leave," he stated politely.

"You don't have to tell me twice," Mikayla told the manager. "These hoes aren't worth my time," she said, throwing up the deuce sign as she walked away. In the background, Mikayla could still hear both Roxy and Ginger talking to one another.

"Let's go," said Ginger.

"Girl, you went off on those bitches, didn't you? We couldn't hear a damn thing you were saying, but your movement told it all," said Jazzman.

"Are you straight, now?" asked Mia.

"C'mon Mia, just because I broke up with Roxy doesn't mean I'm rocking with the other team. You are gonna' have to accept who I am, or you can get tha' hell on, too," stated Mikayla.

"Girl, please, I meant are you straight with everything that has happened with you and Roxy," said Mia.

Roxy's induced drama almost made Mia spill out what she'd heard through the grapevine regarding her sister's fight outside of the strip club. Mia was thinking the whole time that if it wasn't for the respect, she had for Mikayla's privacy, she would have come out and told her sister that she was too good of a person to be dealing with a tramp like Roxy.

"I'm alright," replied Mikayla.

"Well, I'm just glad that you didn't get us kicked tha' fuck out of here," said Jazzman.

"I hope you know that you fucked up my buzz," replied Mia.

"Jazzman…," said Mikayla. "Did you speak with your mama?" she asked in an attempt to lighten the mood. "I was concerned when Aunt Colleen asked me to call you on three-way, and you didn't even pick up for me. I thought we were best of cousins," added Mikayla.

"We are big cuz," responded Jazzman.

"Girl, I wanted her to feel my raft after I caught her with that damn Henry in the restaurant sitting at the bar together," said Jazzman.

"Are you kidding me!?" asked a surprised Mikayla. "That shit sounds like what I just went through with Roxy," she said.

"Well, not quite," said Jazzman. She explained the misunderstanding between what she saw versus what actually happened between her mother and Henry's conversation.

"Well, that's great that y'all were able to work things out," said Mikayla. She was starting to second guess if she'd overreacted to Roxy's conversation with Ginger.

Mikayla couldn't stand the thought of finally losing her woman for good over a meaningless conversation that would make her look like a fool in the end. After hearing Jazzman's story, it made Mikayla want to re-evaluate her actions, which seemed to always show her as an insecure, jealous woman in the eyes of Roxy.

"Isn't Henry the man who used to molest you?" Mia asked bluntly.

"Yes," Jazzman told her cousin, feeling a little awkward about speaking on the topic.

"Mia, don't you have any filter on that mouth of yours," stated Mikayla. "Do you ever think before you speak?" Mikayla asked her sister.

"Why don't you shut up and let me finish," said Mia.

"Jazzman, Henry is dead," she told her cousin. Mia then explained how it happened through the words of her homeboy G-dog.

"Damn, I don't wish death on anyone, but this is some crazy shit," stated Jazzman.

It wasn't at all surprising for Jazzman to hear that Henry was murdered due to his ruthless lifestyle, but it was definitely a shock for his death to come right at a time when he was the cause of her and her mother's recent fallout. Although Jazzman told her cousins that she didn't wish death on anyone, she would be lying if she didn't feel a sense of relief to know that she wouldn't have to ever worry about running into the man she despised on all levels.

Mia wrapped up the bill, and all three women walked out of the *Fun Zone Entertainment Plaza* with a new outlook on life.

Synopsis of Part III

Time heals all wounds. Through time, you see the women in *A Black Girl's Blues* grow. In Part III, Makayla seeks and finds answers to explain her tumultuous relationship with Roxy. She worries if she can handle the outcome of what she finds out.

Colleen realizes that some things happen for a reason as she tries to heal her broken heart from the short-lived marriage with Malcolm. She and her daughter, Jazzman, continue to work on their strained relationship with healing on the horizon.

Mia begins to mend broken relationships—with her mother, her children, and her sister, Makayla. Broken, she finds restoration in becoming a better person and showing love to those most important to her.

The family of women in this fictional story has experienced unimaginable pain, which is relatable to all women in different ways. Parts I - III show how these women worked through broken relationships and made it out of the chaos in their lives.